# THE CIVILIZED WORLD

# THE
# CIVILIZED
# WORLD

## A NOVEL IN STORIES

## SUSI WYSS

A HOLT PAPERBACK   HENRY HOLT AND COMPANY   NEW YORK

Holt Paperbacks
Henry Holt and Company, LLC
*Publishers since 1866*
175 Fifth Avenue
New York, New York 10010
www.henryholt.com

A Holt Paperback® and ® are registered trademarks of
Henry Holt and Company, LLC.

This is a work of fiction. All of the characters, organizations, and events portrayed in
this novel are either products of the author's imagination or are used fictitiously.

"A Modern African Woman" was published in
*Cream City Review* under the title "Comfort," Fall 2009
"Names" appeared in the *Bellingham Review*, Spring 2010
"Waiting for Solomon" appeared in *The Massachusetts Review*, Spring 2010
"Monday Born" appeared in the *Connecticut Review*, Spring 2007

Library of Congress Cataloging-in-Publication Data

Wyss, Susi, 1965–
   The civilized world : a novel in stories / Susi Wyss.
      p. cm.
   ISBN 978-0-8050-9362-9
   1. Women—Fiction.   2. Ghanaians—Fiction.   3. Americans—Ghana—Fiction.
4. Beauty shops—Fiction.   5. Forgiveness—Fiction.   6. Ghana—Fiction.   I. Title.
   PS3623.Y756C58 2011
   813'.6—dc22                                                   2010028288

Henry Holt books are available for special promotions and
premiums. For details contact: Director, Special Markets.

First Edition 2011

Designed by Kelly S. Too

Printed in the United States of America
1   3   5   7   9   10   8   6   4   2

*To my parents,*
*Hans and Edith Wyss*

# CONTENTS

# THE CIVILIZED WORLD

# Monday Born

Adjoa had been going to Madame Janice's every week for the last three months, but she still couldn't put her finger on why her stomach clenched and her shoulders stiffened every time her twin brother, Kojo, drove her to the white woman's well-kept house. Madame Janice was a perfectly pleasant American lady who seemed to appreciate Adjoa's massages. Other than the African masks and statues displayed prominently in the living room, other than the rather rude night watchman, there was really nothing about Madame Janice or her home that could account for Adjoa's anxiety.

Rolling her shoulders in an effort to loosen them, Adjoa guessed her unease had more to do with the drive itself, particularly since it was nighttime and the old car that Kojo often borrowed from a friend made loud clanging noises every time he shifted into a new gear. Abidjan was not the kind of city where two Ghanaians ought to be meandering about in the dark in a clanging car. Kojo knew this as well as

she did—she could tell by his silent concentration, by the
way his eyes narrowed into thin slits as he picked the streets
he drove on, avoiding the ones that were rumored to have
police checkpoints.

Adjoa was often able to read her twin's thoughts, and she
knew, watching him now, that he was thinking about last
week's drive when they'd been pulled over by an Ivoirian
policeman. He'd asked for Kojo's papers, examining them
for so long that Adjoa began to wonder if he could read. He
claimed there was a fine for broken mufflers, a heavy one he
could overlook for the reasonable sum of 1500 CFA francs—
the mere cost of two cold beers. It took fifteen minutes for
Kojo to negotiate him down to 500, and the policeman had
leered at Adjoa as he took the money. *"Beaucoup de graisse,
pas comme les gôs Ivoiriennes,"* he'd muttered appreciatively.
Lots of fat, not like the Ivoirian girls.

Please God don't let us run across one of them tonight,
Adjoa prayed, as the car made its noisy way down the street.
She leaned her head against the headrest and gazed through
her open window at the half-constructed concrete mansions
looming in the darkness—colossal, abandoned structures in
huge lots of overgrown grass. When had it become like this?
Twelve years ago, when they'd come to Abidjan to find
work, Ivoirians had welcomed foreigners, especially to work
as *domestiques* and day laborers. With her beauty-school
degree, she found jobs at various salons, working her way up
to hairdresser at the Hôtel Ivoire. Meanwhile, her brother
found a string of construction jobs in a city that seemed to

expand and grow like the belly of a pregnant woman. The problems seemed to start when President Bédié publicly complained that foreigners were taking jobs from Ivoirians, blaming them for the country's worsening economy. How conveniently he'd overlooked that his own ethnic group, the Baoulé, were Akan people who'd migrated long ago from what was now Ghana.

Adjoa let loose a sigh and leaned her head closer to the window to catch a warm breeze. If only they had enough money saved up to go home. It didn't take an expert to see things were just going to get worse. The bubble of hope following General Guéï's coup d'état last Christmas Eve had already burst. Basic prices were going up, and the rent for their one-room cinder-block house had nearly doubled— their landlord's attempt to either gouge them or get rid of them. Even with all of this, they might have managed if construction hadn't come to a virtual halt and her brother no longer found work.

"Sometimes I wish we could just go home," Kojo said. Adjoa looked at his profile. He had recently taken to wearing his cap backward—a look she'd told him she didn't like. Still, beneath the cap was the same Kojo, the twin who regularly started discussions that joined seamlessly with her trains of thought.

"Soon," she promised. Only a week ago, they'd calculated it would take another six months—if there were no surprises—to save the additional 200,000 CFA they needed to open a beauty salon upon their return to Accra. Over the years, they'd mapped out all the details. Adjoa would be in charge of the beauty treatments, hiring and overseeing staff for routine services like manicures and braiding hair, while providing the more complicated ones herself. Kojo would use his construction skills to transform a rental space and keep it in good working order. He referred to it as an investment, clearly enthralled by the prospect of being his own boss, but Adjoa thought of it differently. She envisioned being known in her community—why not in all of Accra?—for running the best, friendliest, and most reliable salon. Women would come to her exhausted from tending to children, households, and jobs, and they would be treated like queens just long enough to leave refreshed and reenergized. She'd not only be helping other women, she'd also finally be recognized for it.

"You call six months soon? No, Adjoa, we have to find other ways to get money." Kojo turned the car into Riviera III, the neighborhood where Madame Janice lived. The residential street was dark and quiet, with an almost eerie absence of people. "For instance," he continued, "why not ask Madame Janice to pay more for your massages?"

Adjoa shook her head. "I don't know if that's a good idea. She already pays ten thousand for a single hour. That's more than I get paid for a whole day's work at the hotel."

Kojo slowed the car as he turned onto Madame Janice's street. "In my eyes," he said, "it's better to return home with our pockets half full than being shipped back in coffins, all our savings spent on our funerals."

Adjoa turned to give her twin a sharp look, even though

his eyes were still on the road. "Kojo," she said, "where's your good sense? You know better than to say things like that."

"Twelve years in a place like this is enough to chip away at anyone's good sense," he muttered, as he pulled the car to a halt in front of Madame Janice's villa.

"Just remember where we're from, Kojo," Adjoa said. "Remember the hands that fed you." She shouldn't need to remind him that their honest and hardworking family—no matter how poor they might be considered by others—was rich in common sense. Their roots were the one thing that had kept them grounded this far.

Instead of answering her, Kojo leaned back on the head-rest and sighed. Adjoa pulled down the visor and glanced at her reflection in the lighted mirror: a round, makeup-less face, her straightened hair pulled back into a bun. She pat-ted down a few hairs that had come loose in the wind. A God-fearing woman, her brother always called her.

"Will you wait for me here," she asked, "or should I take the *woro woro* home?"

"I'll wait," Kojo said, reaching beneath his legs to pull a small transistor radio from beneath the front seat.

Adjoa raised herself out of the car and shut the door. She carefully brushed at the folds of her dark blue skirt and tugged at the back of her blouse to loosen it where the sweat had glued it to her back. Madame's villa was hidden behind a high cement wall, painted gray and embedded with broken glass on the top to discourage thieves. All along the empty street, similar walls with glass or iron spikes enclosed the other homes. Stray branches of bougainvillea planted on the inside of Madame's garden had escaped and were splayed out like snakes, weighed down by the thick blossoms barely visible in the dark.

When Adjoa rang the doorbell, the security guard, Maurice, called out from the other side of the metal gate, "*Qui est là?*"

"*C'est moi*," she said. "Adjoa."

"*C'est qui, 'Adjoa'?*"

She sighed. As if she hadn't been coming here every Wednesday for a good three months. "*La masseuse.*"

She heard Madame Janice open the sliding door of the living room and call out to the guard to let Adjoa in. As Maurice finally opened the front gate, he took a few steps backward, his arms stretched out as if to protect Madame's red Mercedes-Benz behind him. Adjoa ignored him and walked toward her client.

"Good evening," Adjoa said, clamping her mouth shut before the word *madame* could escape. Janice had told her more than once not to call her that, after which Adjoa stopped calling her anything. *Janice* sounded much too familiar.

"Hi, Adjoa. Come on in," Madame Janice said, waving her into the air-conditioned house and quickly sliding the door shut against the mosquitoes and the sticky, humid night. She wore jeans and a T-shirt, her straight brown hair pulled back into a ponytail, and Adjoa wondered—not for the first time—how old she might be. Her best guess was that she was in her mid-thirties, about the same age as Adjoa.

"You have no idea how badly I need you this week," Janice said. "My neck is in knots, complete knots."

"I'll do my best," said Adjoa.

"I'm sure I'll be putty once you're finished with me. Would you like a glass of water?"

Adjoa shook her head. "No, thank you. I'm ready when you are."

"Okay," Janice answered, turning down the hall toward her bedroom. "I'll call you as soon as I'm ready."

Swathed by the delicious air-conditioned air, Adjoa looked down at the overstuffed sofa and wondered yet again whether she should take the liberty of sitting down. She decided—as she always did—to remain standing.

In three months, all Adjoa had learned about Janice was that she'd lived in Africa for thirteen years, she'd come to the Ivory Coast to work for an American organization, and she lived alone. She tried to glean clues about her client by looking around the living room, but there were no personal photographs, no clutter to reveal whether she had any hobbies or special interests. The living room was a sparsely furnished, wide-open space with a light-gray tiled floor, bright-white walls, and a sweeping archway leading to the dining room. One door led to the kitchen, another led to the hallway toward the bedrooms. Adjoa wasn't sure how many bedrooms there were, but in the past she'd counted

five closed doors when she walked down the hallway to
Madame Janice's bedroom.

It was a large house to live alone in, she thought, even for
a white person. If she herself lived in a place like this, she
would fill it up with family; she didn't have children of her
own yet, but there were plenty of them in her family back
home. Adjoa particularly liked the living room—this was
what she wanted her beauty salon to look like: bright, wide
open, and clean. Not small and cramped and dirty, like the
neighborhood salons where she'd first worked, towels gray
with use and balls of hair gathering in the corners.

Adjoa looked at the shelves against the wall, filled with
carved African statues. As usual, she eyed them suspiciously.
Some of the objects were obviously made for tourists, but
why risk having any of them out in the open? Though Adjoa
was no more superstitious than anyone else she knew, it was
clear that exposing sacred objects was dangerous—an invitation for bad spirits to enter the house. She'd hinted at this
last month, but Madame Janice had missed it entirely, going
on instead about how she enjoyed being surrounded by
souvenirs from all the African countries where she'd lived
over the last thirteen years.

"You must be eager to return home after such a long
time," Adjoa had said, struck by the fact that Janice had been
away from her homeland even longer than she and Kojo had.

But Janice had merely shrugged her shoulders. "I'm used
to moving around a lot," she said. "When I was a kid, my

family moved to a new town every year or two. Besides, the States don't feel like home anymore; it's just a place to visit."

Recalling Janice's words as she waited for her, Adjoa felt sad. Madame Janice had choices—she could live anywhere she wanted, yet she didn't seem to belong anywhere. Adjoa, on the other hand, who knew exactly where her home was, couldn't be there until she had the means to set up a business to provide for herself and her family. How unfair the world sometimes seemed. She scanned Janice's thirteen-year accumulation of souvenirs, finally settling on a matching pair of male and female statues, about twenty centimeters high, with bulging eyes, arms akimbo, and headdresses colored with blue powder. Madame Janice had pointed them out to Adjoa once, referring to them by a name she couldn't recall, and explained that the figures, which represented twins, were carved by the Yoruba in Nigeria, where twins were even more revered than in Ghana. Apparently, when a twin died young, the Yoruba made a statue of the dead twin to house his or her soul, so that the dead twin wouldn't come back to harm the living one.

Why were there two figures? Adjoa wondered. Could it mean that both twins had died? No, she reproached herself, this was not a time for bleak thoughts. She pulled her eyes away from the statues and rested them on an enormous blank TV screen instead. She was relieved when she heard Madame Janice's voice calling her and hurried down the hallway without looking back.

In the bedroom, Adjoa found Janice lying on her back on the bed, dressed in panties with a towel spread underneath her and a bottle of lotion placed on the nightstand. As if readying herself for prayer, Adjoa lowered herself onto her knees at the side of the bed. She poured a pink pool of lotion on her hands, rubbed them together briskly to warm the lotion, and then began to massage the woman's neck and upper chest, feeling the small, pronounced bones beneath the slack skin. She used soft motions, afraid that rubbing the skin too hard, with so little flesh underneath, would leave bruises. As she massaged a shoulder, a sigh swept out of Janice's lungs, like a hushed gust of wind during the small rainy season. After rubbing each arm, Adjoa finished with the hand, the webbing between the thumb and forefinger, and gave each finger a light tug.

Adjoa thought of asking Janice about the twin statues but worried that her employer might wonder why she was looking so closely at things that didn't belong to her. While Janice didn't hesitate to ask Adjoa questions about her, Adjoa didn't feel it was proper to reciprocate. She squirted another dollop of lotion onto her hands and began massaging Janice's stomach and legs. Sometimes, though, she wished she could be as direct as her client. The first day they'd met, Janice had immediately asked her about her name.

"I have two names," Adjoa had explained. "Ataa Adjoa. *Ataa* means female twin, and *Adjoa* means a girl born on a

Monday. I don't use the name Ataa anymore because it confuses people to call my brother and me by similar names; he's called *Ata,* for male twin." She pronounced *Ata* with a short *a* and *Ataa* with a stretched *aa,* even though she knew that Janice's American ear probably couldn't hear the difference. She didn't bother to explain that Kojo had dropped Ata around the same time for the same reason.

"Does being born on a Monday have any special meaning in your culture?" Janice asked.

"It's just our tradition to name children after the day of the week on which they're born, though many people think a person's qualities can be predicted by their name. Monday-borns are said to be quiet."

Janice had smiled and said, "That certainly seems true in your case."

Adjoa finished massaging Janice's feet. She was breathing deeply, as if she were sleeping. Tapping her on the shoulder lightly, Adjoa whispered, "It's time to turn over." With her eyes still closed, Janice turned onto her stomach. This time Adjoa started from the bottom up, the backs of the legs, the buttocks, back, and then neck. Modesty had prevented her from telling Janice the other traits typical of Monday-borns—that they were believed to be hardworking, disciplined, and loyal. Nor did she mention that despite their reputation for being quiet, Monday-borns were not to be taken for granted because they were also strong-willed.

Adjoa felt tight clumps of muscle in Janice's neck and spent at least ten minutes trying to release them. Then she closed the bottle of lotion, tapped her again on the shoulder, and said, "I'll be waiting in the living room."

"This time you have to ask for a raise," Kojo said, his eyes scanning the road ahead of them.

"I know, Kojo." It had been a long week, starting with Kojo going out without his identity card. He'd had the bad luck of taking a bus that was pulled over at a makeshift checkpoint and, with no money to pay off the police, he'd spent several hours in jail. For days afterward he sulked at home, not even bothering to look for work. On top of this, during their weekly phone call home at the nearby *télécentre*, their eldest brother, Kobby, informed them that their mother had been checked into the hospital after what appeared to be a stroke, and they needed money for her care. Adjoa had of course gone immediately to the Western Union office, trying hard not to think of the possibility that she might not see her mother again. Instead, she went over the numbers in her head, counting up their remaining savings, calculating how many more months it would take to save the money they still needed. She already knew that the most they could borrow from the bank in Accra was half the cedi equivalent of the total 2 million CFA they needed. So far, they had saved 800,000 of the remaining million—until last weekend, of course. That had set them back 50,000. Still, with just 250,000 to go, they were so close—couldn't Kojo see that?

"Ask her for fifteen thousand," Kojo said.

"I'm not sure. That's more than anyone I know pays, and I don't want to lose her as a client."

"That woman is plenty rich," he said. "That huge house and no man, no children? Someone like that can throw money away and there's always more. A woman like that has no worries."

Without looking at her brother, Adjoa knew what he was thinking. Their neighbor's boss was selling his old luxury sedan, and Kojo had gone to see it this weekend. It had been pointless; she'd said so to him the same night. It made no sense that he would still be contemplating that car, but she knew with complete certainty, the way she always knew when she could read his mind, that he was picturing himself right now, driving it. For a moment Adjoa wished their money troubles would just go away. What would it be like to live in a villa like Madame's and not have family worries or money worries? Then she wondered: How did Kojo know Madame Janice lived alone? She couldn't recall telling him.

"Maybe I could ask for twelve thousand," she said.

"Fifteen," Kojo insisted, as he pulled the car over in front of Janice's house. He turned off the ignition and looked at Adjoa, his eyebrows raised in an expression that she knew only too well. How many times had he used it as a boy, to coax her into sharing a handful of groundnuts or her half of an orange after he'd already eaten his? Even then, she had never refused him.

"Look," Kojo said. "We need another two hundred fifty

thousand CFA. If you get the raise and we save everything you get from her, we'll have enough in seventeen weeks. That's four months, Adjoa, and that's all I can take of this place."

Though his numbers matched the ones Adjoa had been calculating in her head, she was unsure what to make of the tone of his voice.

"What do you mean, that's all you can take?"

"Just that. I refuse to stay here longer than four months, and I'm not leaving without enough money to start the business. I don't care anymore what it's going to take."

Adjoa's heartbeat quickened; Kojo had never talked like this before. "What are you saying, brother?"

"I'm saying this city has easy and fast ways to make money," he said. "I'm saying there are people like your madame who are so rich they wouldn't even notice if some of their things should disappear."

Adjoa stared at her brother. "That's not you talking," she said. "I don't know who it is, but it's not my twin."

"Open your eyes, Adjoa. We're living in a city where nobody gives a damn if we live or die. The only people who can take care of us are us."

Adjoa knew that Kojo was as worried as she was about their mother, that he was still angry about his run-in with the police. He didn't mean what he was saying. "You're just upset," she said. "I know it's hard for you when there's not much work to be found, Kojo. Please don't worry. I'll ask for the raise."

She lifted herself out of her seat and shut the door. Leaning into the open window, she added, "We're so close, Kojo. We just need to hang on a few more months."

Kojo shrugged his shoulders and slumped down in his seat, their conversation clearly unfinished. But Adjoa didn't know what else to say, so she walked to the front gate and rang the doorbell. Before Maurice could ask who it was, she called out, "*C'est Adjoa, la masseuse.*"

He opened the gate a tiny notch, and she saw his dark eyes peering out at her, like a lizard's staring at a fly that is about to become his lunch. When Adjoa asked him if Madame was there, he answered yes but gave no indication of opening the gate.

What are you waiting for? Adjoa thought. Let me in. She heard Janice's voice in the background. "*Maurice, c'est Adjoa?*"

Maurice kept the entry shut, his lizard eyes fixed on Adjoa as he tilted his head to the side to shout over his shoulder, "*Oui, madame.*"

Only when Madame Janice told him to let her inside did he finally open the gate, turning his back to Adjoa as if she were no longer of any interest to him. Janice stood beyond the threshold, wearing a thin pale-blue robe embroidered with bright flowers. In the dim light, the fabric shimmered like smooth, flowing water, as if to remind Adjoa that she would never own something as elegant or as expensive as this.

When Adjoa left Janice's house an hour later, Maurice was not in his usual place seated on a straw mat in the carport. At the sound of his voice on the other side of the wall, she opened the front gate herself. Outside, Maurice was leaning into the driver's window of her brother's car, the two men talking in low voices. Adjoa marched to the passenger side and climbed into her seat.

"I'm back, Kojo. Let's go." She looked past her brother at the night watchman. "*Bonne nuit, Maurice,*" she said, her voice sounding shrill to her ears.

Kojo and Maurice nodded at each other wordlessly, and Kojo started the car and pulled out onto the street.

"What were the two of you talking about?" she asked him.

"Nothing. Man talk."

"Man talk?"

"You know," he said. "Man talk. Sports and such. How did it go?"

"Fine, Kojo. She agreed to the raise."

He seemed to mull this over, his head and shoulders hunched, his hands gripping the steering wheel as he navigated the car across a speed bump—*gendarme couché* or reclining policeman, the Ivoirians called them. Adjoa watched him for several minutes, trying to translate his body language.

"Kojo," she finally asked, "what are you thinking about?" She realized as the words came from her mouth that she had never had to ask her twin brother this question before.

"Nothing," he said, without looking over. "Nothing you need to worry about."

But Adjoa kept her eyes locked on Kojo. Except for the backward cap on his head, he appeared no different from the boy who had come with her to Abidjan twelve years ago, the brother who had always tried to protect her, the twin who shared her every thought. And yet she couldn't help but wonder: Who is this person next to me? Where is the brother I used to know as well as I know myself?

She shook her head and took a deep breath. If they could just make it through the next four months and get home, certainly they would be all right and Kojo would be his old self again. Then she peered out into the darkness of the city—a place that would always remain dark in her mind—and she wasn't sure of anything anymore.

# Names

## Nobody

The plumber doesn't tell me his name, even though it's the first thing I want to ask, a compulsion as sudden as the rush of hot Malawian air that follows him inside before I slide the glass door shut. Only later, after I've led him to the bathroom and watched him stoop to peer into the toilet tank, do I decide that enough time has passed for me to ask.

Tall and well-built, his dark face still glistening from the heat outside, he looks up at me and answers, "Nobody," with a shrug of his shoulders. For a second I wonder if he's being rude—if he doesn't want to answer my question, he should just say so—until I grasp that his name really is Nobody. I sit down on the edge of the tub, willing my hands to stay still in my lap as I deliberate over the gift of a new name to add to my notebook.

"Where does your name come from?" I ask, in as casual

a tone as I can muster, hoping he'll give me a story to tell Philip tonight.

But there is no story. "My grandmother named me," he answers. "I don't know why she chose Nobody. She named my younger sister Somebody."

I lean closer toward him. "Does your sister live in Lilongwe, too?"

"Yes, madam. She works at your embassy. It's through her that I found this job," he explains, his voice so devoid of enthusiasm that I'm not sure what to say next.

He wipes his hands on a rag, which he throws into his toolbox before closing it with a loud snap. "I found the problem but I need a part to fix it. I'll fetch money from the embassy to buy it and return later today."

After he leaves, I pull out the notebook that I use to record peculiar local names and carefully spell it out: Nobody.

When we first came to Malawi, names were a recurring topic of conversation at dinner with Philip. Most Malawians, we learned, are given two names—one in English and another in the local language. Sometimes the English ones are plain Christian names, but other times they're unusual, even amusing, like Philip's embassy colleague, Address, and the government official he met who was named Square. We tried to guess where these strange names came from, made up silly stories to explain them. When he came home with the news that they'd hired a new driver named Tonic, I joked that he probably had a twin named Gin. Philip never asks these people about their names when he meets them. He claims it would be rude and culturally insensitive, though I don't agree; who doesn't want to tell their story if they have one to tell? But then, that is like Philip; he's never been one to talk about himself and he assumes the rest of the world feels the same.

Lilongwe would not have been my choice for a first posting, but Philip explained the need to prove himself before he could be assigned to a European embassy. I'd never had any interest in going to Africa, but I was excited about being a foreign-service wife. I fancied myself the vital anchor, lowered anew at every port, ensuring a safe and happy haven for our family-to-be. A kind of international Martha Stewart. Before our trip, I bought *The Taste of Home Cookbook* and *101 Family Craft Projects*. Then, in a frenzied afternoon of shopping two days before the movers came, I added a bread-making machine, a state-of-the-art Cuisinart, a handcrafted Amish quilting frame, and a sewing machine imported from Switzerland. I stuffed four shopping bags with oil paints and brushes, colorful packets of mismatched glass beads, and papers and stickers for a scrapbook that would capture our adventures.

When we first arrived, I took my projects seriously. I taught our cook, Rose, how to make elaborate four-course meals. I painted a series of still lifes of the bougainvillea that grew along our seven-foot-high fence, until I'd depleted my supply of magenta paint. I convinced Philip to take me to Mvuu Camp, snapping hundreds of pictures and gluing only the best ones into the scrapbook—shots of sable antelopes, brown-breasted barbets, and elephants bathing in the Shire River. I formed a quilting bee with other expat women, sewing bright African cloth into patterns with names like Morning Star, Patience Corner, and Bright Hopes. One of them still hangs on the bedroom wall as a testament to my initial enthusiasm, my steadfast belief in our new life.

I realize now, eighteen months after our arrival here and, most likely, according to Philip, another eighteen before we leave, that I was nesting, creating a home for the real project—our baby. In preparation for my pregnancy, I took care of myself. On temperate days, I played tennis and rode horses at the Lilongwe Golf Club. In the hot months, I jogged on the treadmill in one of our extra bedrooms, cranking up the air-conditioning, much to the pleasure of Cooper, our Labrador retriever, who sheds about a pound of hair a day when the heat is sweltering. And finally I gave up drinking beer, even though Malawian Carlsberg, advertised in cautious superlative as "probably the best beer," was one of the few things that tasted like home.


At dinner, I tell Philip about Nobody, even though there's nothing to tell, really, since there's no explanation for the grandmother's choice of name.

"It makes you think, doesn't it?" I add. "About the power of names, I mean. How a name like that can leave a psychological imprint. It can hardly be a coincidence that Nobody is less successful than his sister Somebody. After all, they come from the same family, so it can't have been their upbringing."

"I suppose you're right, Ophelia," Philip answers, clearly distracted as he dabs at his goatee with a napkin. Even though he's been growing it for more than a month, I still haven't gotten used to the contrast of those coarse, dark hairs against his pale face. "But more importantly," he asks, as he places the napkin back on his lap, "did he fix the toilet?"

"Actually, no. He had to get a part and didn't come back."

"I'll be sure to mention it at the embassy tomorrow," he says, eating another forkful of the beef stew Rose has prepared, a recipe I've taught her, that I've watched her follow exactly down to the pinch of salt. Somehow it never tastes as good as when I used to make it, even though the ingredients— ripe tomatoes, fresh parsley, onions, and garlic—look the same as back home.

We spend the rest of the meal in silence—what Philip would call a companionable silence. He is by nature an introvert—the main reason we never entertain and only attend embassy functions when he says it's important. In the last few months, I've finally come to understand what his mother meant when she told me, shortly after our engagement, that Huffington men aren't talkers. Even so, I can't help but wonder, when he tells me that he's thankful for the respite he finds at home, whether this isn't just a nice way of telling me: Don't bring me your problems or ours.

Nobody doesn't come back the next day or the next. When the embassy finally sends another plumber three days later to finish fixing the toilet, he's an older, heavyset man who, when I ask for his name, tells me it's George.

## Why

I watch the girl, her hair cropped neatly against her scalp, sitting on a stool in the front yard and petting Cooper while she waits for her mother, our cook Rose. She is the first Malawian child I've met who isn't afraid of our dog, and I guess her to be about eight years old. When Rose let slip last week that her youngest daughter was named Why, I couldn't resist asking her to bring the child over so I could see what she looks like. All six of the girl's older siblings, it turns out, have boring Christian names.

The introduction to Why was embarrassing—she curtsied with one knee on the ground and stayed there until I told her to get up—and there is nothing in her demeanor as I watch her pet the dog that explains her name.

I go into the kitchen to find Rose.

"Why Why?" I ask her, then suddenly realize she might think I'm stuttering. "I mean, how did you choose your daughter's name?"

"She wasn't planned," Rose explains, looking down at the floor as she always does when she addresses me. "We took *precautions*." She pronounces the last word slowly, a term clearly reserved for this one topic—the story of why Why.

"We followed the nurse's advice, but I became pregnant anyway. That's why my husband named her Why."

Later, I watch through the window as Rose leaves with Why, the smell of her chicken-and-rice dish simmering on the stove. Cooper follows the girl to the front gate, wagging his tail as if he wants to leave with her. For the rest of the day I carry around an image of Why petting the dog, along with the sound of her name, of my question, echoing in my head: Why Why? I wonder if her name is spelled with or without a question mark. At first, I'm eager for Philip to come home so I can tell him about her curious name, but as I mull over the story behind it, the randomness and injustice of it all, I decide not to share it with him after all.

Instead, I open my notebook. Beneath Address, Square, Tonic, Spoon, Express, Surprise, Nobody, and Somebody, I add: Why. Then I reread the list of names, notice how crooked some of the letters are, and decide to rewrite the whole list on a fresh sheet of paper, keeping the letters contained in symmetrically printed lines.

Until recently, I used to break up my days by visiting Philip at his office at noon, bringing him his lunch in a colorful basket I found at the market soon after we moved here. He always greeted me with a kiss and talked to me while he ate, but eventually he had less and less time to spend with me when I delivered his lunches. He explained they were short-staffed at his office, but whatever the reason he also started working later in the evenings. If I didn't know him as well as I do, I'd suspect an affair. But it's not lost on me that his busyness started right after we returned from our home leave three months ago.

A few weeks ago in October, when the hot season had just begun, I waited for him in the lobby for a good ten minutes. Finally, feeling restless, I stepped into the heat, venturing out of the compound just beyond the security checkpoint. Across the street, a young woman, her head scarf and dress a drab shade of brown, stood talking in Chichewa to one of the local staff with an embassy badge hanging from a cord around his neck. She held a basket, a replica of my own, filled with little knit booties and caps for babies in very un-African shades of pastel pink and blue and yellow. Even as part of me wanted to turn away, I felt myself taking a step toward her, as if the colorful contents of her basket were tugging at me. I thought of my pregnant sister back home, how I'd procrastinated long enough in sending a gift for her baby shower.

"How much do they cost?" I asked the woman, realizing as the words came from my mouth that I didn't have any kwacha with me.

"Not expensive, madam," she answered, pushing the basket toward me.

"Actually, I forgot to bring money," I said. Behind me,

one of the guards called out that Philip's secretary, Eunice, was looking for me.

"Next time then," she said, placing the basket on her head.

Inside the compound, Eunice was motioning to me. "Your husband is ready to see you now," she informed me, as I entered the air-conditioned lobby. The long wait and the heat had made me irritable, but the thought of climbing the stairs to Philip's office to receive his scratchy-bearded kiss on my cheek, to talk about how much work he had or how insufferable the weather had become—in short, any topic but the one I wanted to discuss—incensed me even more.

I handed Eunice the basket without a word and turned to walk back to my car, trying my best to tune out her voice as she called after me, "Mrs. Hullington, are you all right?"

Now I spend my days puttering around the house, tidying up and establishing order in my new life. At first it was a matter of putting away half-started projects and sorting though craft supplies. I folded up the unfinished quilt, disassembled the quilt frame, and stowed away the sewing machine. For two days, I organized all of the beads into separate glass jars, sorting them by size and color and arranging the jars on a shelf so that they formed a rainbow of reds, oranges, yellows, greens, blues, and indigos. I hung and rehung the bougainvillea paintings on the living room walls so they were perfectly straight and spaced and then decided to give them all away, preferring the walls to be pure white.

Every laundry day, I reiron and refold our clothes. Even though I've shown the houseboy several times how to iron Philip's shirts and fold our clothes so the creases are straight and symmetrical, the socks in tight bundles, he never puts the same care into it that I do. Then I arrange all our clothes by color in the closet and drawers.

For a few weeks the women from the quilting bee and the golf club left messages on my cell phone, inviting me for tea or tennis. But I knew if I confided in them, Philip and I would have been ground into a million pieces by the rumor mill. I never called back, and the phone has stopped ringing.

Lately, I've been preoccupied by my search for the best place to keep my notebook of names—someplace where I can be sure it won't be lost or stolen. But I still haven't found the right spot, so I carry it around with me, always safely in my hands or at my side, as I move from room to room. At night when I place it on my nightstand, I can feel Philip watching me, but he never asks to see what's inside.

### Grief

I'm sorting through the china, stacking paper towels between them so that they're less likely to chip, when Grief appears. My notebook is next to the roll of thick, highly absorbent towels shipped through diplomatic pouch. I am so intent on my task that I'm startled when Ken, the guard, raps on the metal frame of the sliding door, motioning to me through the glass.

"A woman," he says, "come to see you, madam. I didn't like to disturb you but she says you know her."

When I ask for her name, he tells me Grief. I have no idea who the person is, but I can't resist. I need to see what Grief looks like.

It turns out that I *do* know her—the woman from outside the embassy selling baby booties and caps. She explains she came because she didn't see me again at the embassy. Lord knows how she found my house; I guess they all know where we live.

As with Nobody, I want to ask Grief about her name right away, but I tell myself I need to wait. The urge is so strong that I scratch myself instead, raking my fingernails against both of my upper arms. Basket in hand, she stares at me, her head tilted to the side. When I invite her to step inside, she follows me into the living room. I sit cross-legged on the sofa and motion for her to take one of the overstuffed chairs, but with a sideways glance at Cooper sprawled at my feet, she tells me she prefers to stand.

I feign interest in the baby clothes, telling myself I'll finally buy something for my sister. Reaching for a pair of butter-colored booties, I begin to examine them for lost stitches or imperfections, when I hear my voice, as if someone else is speaking, asking this woman why her name is Grief.

"I was christened something else," she answers matter-of-factly, seemingly undaunted by my question. She doesn't mention what her original name was, and I don't ask. "So many sad things have happened to me, that I finally started telling people to call me Grief."

I ask her—I can't stop myself—what some of those things are.

"When I was eleven, my parents died in a minibus accident." I nod, waiting for more. "I became pregnant a few years later. I was still a child myself. A schoolmate told me about an herbalist. . . ."

Her eyes shift to the ground as Rose's did when she told me about Why. "I had her take the pregnancy out."

In the ensuing stillness, I look down at the pair of yellow booties nestled in my hands, as soft and perfect as two newborn chicks. They tremble imperceptibly with the rise and fall of my chest. When Grief finally breaks the silence, her voice is a mere whisper. "Something went wrong inside," she says. "I can't have children now."

I raise my head and look at her, really look at her, taking in the round, unsmiling face, the sad downward tilt of her eyes. I wonder: How did *she* learn the news? I think of being probed in the doctor's examination room during our recent home leave, how icy cold it was even though a parade of naked women expose themselves to him there daily. And then, sitting in the doctor's office, listening to him use terms like *cervical mucus*, *abnormalities*, and *infertility* as casually as if he were saying coffee, cream, and sugar. Philip's hand felt warm and clammy in my freezing-cold one, as if he were already back in Africa, far away from the overly air-conditioned office.

As Grief finishes her story, explaining how she learned to knit for other people's babies, my eyes wander to the notebook of names on the side table. The first page holds a list of baby names that I know by heart, penned in a loose, easy script more than a year ago, bright and cheery names like Daisy, Angelina, Lily, and Claire—all for girls since we'd already decided on Philip for a boy. How different those names were from the Malawian ones I added later—names I used to think were so strange but that I realize now are amazingly apt for my unconceivable child: Nobody, Why, and, now, Grief.

I place the booties onto the side table and reach out for my notebook. Only this time, it's more out of habit than longing, and my hand stops in midair and falls back, empty, into my lap. I decide that I can wait to include her name, that maybe when I add it, the list will even be complete—ready for me to show to Philip, whether he wants to look at it or not.

But none of that matters now. All that exists is the space between Grief and me. She watches me, expectantly. The room is so quiet I can hear Cooper's steady breathing at my feet. Where will I find the right words, what can I possibly say? Because someway, somehow, I need to convince her to stay, to sit with me in a vigil for the unnamed.

# A Modern African Woman

During her layover in London, halfway between Accra and Washington, D.C., Comfort gazed across the black tarmac at the overcast sky, the mounds of dirty snow, and shivered despite the well-heated indoors. For a panicked moment, she wondered what she would do if her son wasn't at Dulles Airport to receive her. But she pushed the thought away firmly, settling instead into a familiar sense of longing for her husband, Kwaku. Though he'd never been far from her thoughts since his death six months ago, Kwaku's absence felt especially painful during this journey—her first time overseas to visit their son.

Landing at Dulles nine hours later, Comfort was relieved to see there was no snow. She was doubly reassured—once she'd navigated customs and retrieved her bags—to see her son, Ekow, standing next to his wife, Linda, who carried their baby against her stomach in a pouch. Almost like an African woman, Comfort thought approvingly, except of course the baby wasn't tied against her back, and Linda was white.

In the car, Comfort's son leaned his right arm against the ledge between their seats, holding the steering wheel with just his left hand, looking ahead at the road as he asked after each of his brothers and sisters. He appeared at ease and relaxed in this white man's country, and Comfort stifled a bubble of pride as it rose in her chest, knowing quite well what comes after pride.

After answering Ekow's questions about the family and letting him know everyone was doing well, Comfort looked out at the scenery and noticed the trees. Although a few of them were still healthy and green, most were leafless and gray. She asked Ekow why he hadn't mentioned on the phone that there was a drought.

"A drought, Mum?"

"The trees, Ekow. Most of them are quite dead."

Comfort heard a chuckle from Linda in the backseat. "The trees aren't dead," Ekow explained. "This is winter. They lose their leaves with the cold, but as soon as the air warms up in a few months, the leaves will come back again."

In Ghana, Comfort had seen near-dead trees come back to life with some good watering, but not once had they come back after they'd lost every one of their leaves. Surely her son was being overly optimistic.

"It's like they're sleeping, Comfort," Linda added, pulling herself forward to lean between Comfort and Ekow, using her mother-in-law's first name as if they were old schoolmates.

Comfort bit her lip and looked over at Ekow, who kept his eyes on the road as he shifted his right hand to the steering wheel to grip it with both hands.

"It's an interesting observation, though," Linda continued. "I've never thought of it, but they do look sort of dead, don't they? It'll be so fascinating, Comfort, to have your perspective in our lives."

The next day, Comfort watched her American daughter-in-law bathe the baby, Amanda, in a yellow plastic tub set inside the kitchen sink. It seemed awkward, standing in front of the tub to hold Amanda with one hand, using the other to dab at her tiny body with a washcloth. Comfort had always bathed her children—and now her grandchildren—the Ghanaian way: seated on a low stool, the baby balanced across her legs stretched over a large flat basin of water. She massaged their joints and ankles before giving them a thorough sponge bath with soap and water. More often than not the babies cried out in protest—otherwise, they weren't getting clean; she might just as well have dipped them in water and dried them off.

Linda lifted Amanda out of the water gingerly, as if she were a delicate bird that would be crushed by the lightest pressure. Everything about Linda, too, seemed fragile—her small, slender figure, the fine features of her face framed by wispy strands of dark brown hair. Comfort fought the urge to reach in and take over from her daughter-in-law—something that her own mother-in-law, who'd been half Fante and half Ashanti, would have done without hesitation. Instead, she reminded herself that there could be more than one way to accomplish a task, even if the new way didn't make much sense. Though it had always been the way of the Fante for mothers-in-law to control their sons and boss around their daughters-in-law, she, Comfort Efua Kwantsima, was a modern African woman, able to hold her tongue in the same situations where her mother-in-law had not. After all, she was an educated person who'd made it to standard seven and represented a new generation.

Linda placed Amanda on a towel on the kitchen counter. Watching her daughter-in-law put a disposable nappy on Amanda and dress her in a striped jumpsuit, Comfort tried unsuccessfully to recall her own children's tiny bodies. They had all grown taller than she was and were now making children of their own. Comfort felt a twinge in her right knee, as if her body were reminding her that she was an old woman now. She lowered herself onto one of the metal chairs by the kitchen table.

Linda raised Amanda into her arms and handed her to Comfort while she poured the bathwater out of the plastic tub and placed the tub on the kitchen counter. Taking a second seat, she grabbed a mug from the table and took a sip. She made a grimace. "Cold coffee—I never get to finish a fresh cup anymore. Then again," she said, slumping forward, placing her elbow on the table and cupping her chin with her hand, "I probably shouldn't drink it anyway. I'm not getting enough sleep as it is."

It was the first time since her arrival that Linda had said anything to her that sounded personal, anything more than a few stilted interjections into Comfort and Ekow's conversations. "It will get easier," Comfort answered, shifting Amanda so that she lay on her back. "Soon she'll start sleeping through the night."

"Even when she's asleep," Linda said in a high-pitched voice, her fingers fidgeting with the handle of the mug, "I'm so worried about her I can't sleep."

With her hunched figure dressed in a thick sweater and jeans, the nails of her restless hands bitten to the quick, Linda looked to Comfort like a child, even though she was in her late twenties, the same age as Ekow. "I was worried with my first baby, too," Comfort told her, though she didn't remember being particularly anxious, just terribly busy. Comfort's mother-in-law had been the strongest presence in her household, but her mother and sisters had been a great help in the first months, stopping by the house almost every day. Comfort wondered about Linda's family—she knew from her son that they hadn't attended the small civil wedding. Ekow had met them only once, a fact he'd confided to Comfort when he came home for his father's funeral, hinting that Linda's family hadn't been entirely pleased about their marriage.

Linda reached out her hand to stroke Amanda's wisps of black hair. "It just doesn't seem fair that I have to leave her with you just as she's getting interesting," she said, her voice faltering.

"She'll be fine with me," said Comfort, as she adjusted her thighs under the bundle.

"Of course, she will. I didn't mean. . . ." Linda pulled back her hand. "Of course, we appreciate you coming here for these six months. It's just . . . well, I guess I don't feel ready to go back to work just yet."

"Then wait a bit longer before you return to work," Comfort said, looking up at her daughter-in-law.

Linda looked away and stood up abruptly. "Yeah, right, with our mortgage?" she said, carrying her mug to the sink and dropping it with a loud clatter.


The next morning, Ekow and Linda rushed about the house, preparing to leave for work. Seated at the kitchen table with Amanda in her lap, Comfort watched her son hastily prepare a sandwich for his lunch, thinking how it would never have been enough to satisfy his midday appetite when he'd been a boy.

"Hurry, Peter, or I'll be late for my nine o'clock," Linda called out, using Ekow's Christian name. Maybe if Ekow hadn't had to wait so long for Linda to finish in the bathroom before he could use it, he would have been ready by now. Comfort waited for him to say something in answer to his wife, but without a word he shoved his sandwich into a bag and took a step toward the hallway. As if suddenly remembering that she was there, he turned to his mother and smiled. "Good-bye, Mummy," he said. "I'll ring you later to see how you're coming along."

Ekow had always been the quietest—and the least confrontational—of her boys. Of course he was a Thursday-born child, who tended to be calm, certainly calmer than Ato, her first, and Mensah, the third boy. He'd been even quieter than his younger sisters, preferring to listen rather than talk, always with his nose in a book, studying. Comfort smiled back at her son and rose from her seat to accompany him, carrying Amanda in her arms.

Linda stood next to the front door, pulling a heavy coat over her gray silk jacket and matching trousers. She leaned in to rub her nose against Amanda's. "Bye-bye, sweetie pie," she said, wiggling the tips of her fingers at her daughter, "Mommy's gonna miss you *so* much."

She looked up at Comfort as Ekow opened the door. "Just call me on my cell if there's anything, anything at all," she said.

"Yes, of course," Comfort promised.

As Linda pushed open the storm door, a gust of cold air blew inside. Ekow dashed after her, giving Comfort just enough time to say in Fante, "Walk well, Ekow," before he flashed another smile and shut the front door. She listened to the sounds of their shoes—the sharp clicking of Linda's heels, the heavier thud of her son's feet—as they strode down the stone path. She stood still, listening to the car doors slam, the engine start, and the car drive off. Except for the humming of the refrigerator from the kitchen, she heard only silence, a silence so profound that she could hear the baby's heartbeat against her bosom, a beat that was replicated in a slower rhythm by her own heart.

As any good grandmother would do, one of the first things Comfort had examined, once she had had a thorough look at her granddaughter, was the shape of her head. It was not bad, the right size for a child who had clearly taken on her father's intelligence, but her forehead jutted out in a way that would need to be rounded out. Even though Amanda was already three months old, there was sufficient time to remold it, about another year before the baby's fontanel closed up, making any further shaping impossible.

Alone in the house for the first time with her granddaughter, Comfort brought her into the kitchen and filled a bowl with warm water from the tap. She pulled a towel from the rack next to the refrigerator and draped it over her shoulder. Carrying Amanda with one arm and the bowl with the other, she walked to the living room and placed the bowl on the coffee table as she sat down on the couch. She dipped the towel into the water, wrung it out tightly, and applied the warm cloth against the baby's skull, pushing ever so gently against the forehead, following the same technique that Comfort had used with her own children, exactly as her mother-in-law had instructed her so many years ago. Dunking the cloth into the water and wringing it out again, Comfort softly wiped outward against each of Amanda's cheeks to broaden her face. The baby blinked twice at the washcloth so close to her face and stared up at her grandmother with large dark-brown eyes.

With Amanda nestled in her lap, Comfort closed her eyes and listened again to the unnerving quiet of the empty house. Back home, there were always people about—the grandchildren who were too young for school, a daughter-in-law or two, the neighbors stopping by on random visits. The house help, too, were always underfoot and needing instructions. What would she do by herself with the baby all day? With a determined nod of her head, she opened her eyes. They would go to the park, she decided. Maybe a mother would be there with her children or, better yet, another grandmother.

As she dressed Amanda in a thick brown jacket with a hood that had an embroidered nose and eyes, Comfort wondered what animal it was supposed to resemble. Not that it mattered—her granddaughter looked so endearing that she stopped for a moment, gazing at her, amazed that this baby, the color of melted sugar, belonged to her family. Then she pushed her own arms into the sleeves of the new coat Ekow had purchased for her and wrapped a wool scarf about her neck. Now where was the key? Ah, on the table in the hallway. Once they were outside, she placed the baby in the pram her son had left there and turned to lock the house.

Walking the five blocks to the park in the cold air, sticking to the route that Ekow and Linda had shown her the day before, Comfort felt a stiffness in her joints. She'd grown used to her mild arthritis back in Ghana, but the cold air seemed to worsen it. A gust of wind swirled around her, biting her face. A cluster of dried dead leaves danced in circles on the street, making a startling scratching sound against the asphalt. She stopped in the middle of the street, as if paralyzed. How could a pile of dead leaves make so much noise?

A row of bare trees lined the street, their branches reaching into the sky like hundreds of arms locked in an act of surrender. Could Ekow possibly be right that they weren't dead? Comfort glanced down at her granddaughter in the pram and felt a flicker of warmth in her chest. No matter how lonely she felt in this strange country, she would stay for Amanda and Ekow—at least long enough to see if he was right about the trees.

The park was empty except for a middle-aged woman seated on a bench and dressed in a woolen hat, jeans, and a puffy gray jacket. A small tawny dog, carrying a red ball in its mouth, ran toward the woman. As a rule, Comfort was wary of dogs—she found them to be dangerous at worst and dirty at best. She watched the woman pull the ball from the dog's mouth and fling it across the park, which propelled the animal forward like a speeding car. Comfort decided that if the woman could reach into the dog's mouth, it was likely to fall under the dirty category rather than the dangerous one, and she wheeled the pram to the bench and sat down on the other end.

"Hello," she said. "I'm Comfort."

The woman stared at her for a moment and then smiled, the wrinkles around her eyes seeming to dance. She was older than Comfort had initially thought.

"What a great name you have," the lady said. "Mine's Gerrie. I haven't seen you here before." The dog sprinted up to her, and she leaned down to take the ball, once again throwing it to the other end of the park.

"I just arrived," Comfort said. "I'm from Ghana. I'm here to visit my son and take care of my grandchild."

"He's very cute," said Gerrie. "You must be proud."

It was Comfort's turn to be confused. Did this woman know her son? Did Americans refer to grown men as cute? Then she noticed that Gerrie was gazing into the pram.

"Amanda's a girl," Comfort explained, "not a boy." No one had ever mistaken any of her baby girls as boys, but she had always followed the Ghanaian custom of having their ears pierced within a week or two of birth. She looked at her granddaughter, her round face framed by the hood of her jacket, her earlobes visibly naked and unpierced.

"Oh, sorry. *She's* cute." Gerrie corrected herself. "I have three grandsons myself, but they live on the West Coast with their parents. I see them once a year if I'm lucky."

How sad for Gerrie to be such a long way off from her children and grandchildren. Comfort thought of her own family, so far away in Ghana. But before she could find the right consoling words, Gerrie stood up abruptly, her attention focused on something across the park. Comfort looked in the same direction and quickly turned away again—the dog was crouching, easing himself. Gerrie jammed her hands into the pockets of her jacket and pulled out a blue plastic bag.

"Well," she said, "gotta pick up after Wally. Welcome to the neighborhood. I hope I'll see you around."

"Yes," Comfort said. "I hope so, too."

Gerrie walked toward the spot where the dog had been crouching and stooped down. Comfort watched with dismay as the woman scooped up the dog's feces with the plastic bag and carried the bag over to a nearby rubbish bin. The dog had already sauntered off, ball clamped in his jaw, ears flapping and tail wagging, Gerrie following behind. Comfort wondered who the true master was—the woman or her dog—and whether she would ever understand these Americans with their strange customs.

When Linda returned from work that evening, she rushed to Amanda, plucking her from Comfort's arms. After firing off questions about Amanda's bodily functions and napping schedule, and apparently satisfied with the answers, Linda disappeared into the nursery with her. Comfort went into the kitchen to finish preparing that night's meal of spicy groundnut soup, which she planned to serve with fufu made from one of the boxes of Instant Neat powder she'd brought in her suitcase. Once Linda, who'd never been to Ghana, was properly introduced to Ghanaian cooking, Comfort planned to show her how to prepare it herself so she could make Ekow's favorite meals after Comfort left. And of course eventually for Amanda, too, so she would learn to love her country's food as much as her father.

They had wanted to visit—at one point Ekow had even mentioned they might have their wedding in Accra—but that notion had been cast aside when Linda got pregnant. Not that she would have been the first pregnant bride, nor would it have shocked Comfort's family for them to marry after the baby was born. But Ekow had explained over the phone that Linda preferred a quick, simple ceremony attended by a few friends. When Ekow came home three months later for his father's funeral, he said that Linda couldn't travel while she was pregnant, because of the risk of malaria.

When Ekow appeared a half hour later, he came straight to the kitchen and complimented the smell of Comfort's cooking before he climbed the stairs to bring his wife down for supper. At the table, Linda held Amanda in her lap as Comfort asked her son about his workday selling cars at a Honda dealership. He described the different clients who came in to look at cars, how he could never tell from looking at them which ones were in debt until he ran a credit check on his computer. Comfort liked to think about her son being the gateway to so many people buying cars. As he talked,

Linda pushed the food around her plate, leaning in to kiss Amanda's head every few minutes.

When Ekow asked Comfort about her day, she told him about meeting Gerrie at the park. Then she added casually, "Don't you think you should pierce Amanda's ears? She'd look so pretty with small gold hoops."

Linda looked up from her plate, but it was Ekow who answered. "Mummy, sometimes American girls wait until they're teenagers before they pierce their ears."

"But she's Ghanaian, too," Comfort said.

"Of course she is," Linda said. "It's just that we can't bear to hurt her in any way."

"If they pierce their ears as teenagers it hurts just as much," Comfort reasoned, "but if you do it when they're babies, they won't remember."

"How do you *know* they don't remember?" Linda asked, her voice rising slightly.

Comfort turned to Ekow. "Do you remember anything that happened to you when you were three months old?"

Ekow shrugged. "I suppose not, Mum."

Linda looked at Ekow, her mouth forming a thin, straight line. "All the same," she said, "we don't intend to pierce Amanda's ears."

Comfort paused. She could see that Linda's mind was set, but she also knew that her daughter-in-law's thinking was contrary to Amanda's well-being. "But children are *supposed* to learn that life is hard," she finally explained. "It's a parent's duty to teach them that suffering and happiness are twins."

Linda carefully placed her napkin on the table. "I think I know what my duty is," she replied, pushing her chair back and scraping it against the wood floor. Holding Amanda in one arm, she stood up, used her free hand to collect her dishes, and disappeared into the kitchen.

Comfort bit her lip at Linda's rudeness—Comfort would never have considered speaking this way to her own mother-in-law, never mind walking out of the room. Not that she was comparing, of course. She looked over at her son.

"Sorry about that, Mum," he said. "Linda's been somewhat anxious lately."

"Anxious? But why?"

He looked down at his half-finished plate. "She's always been a little . . . like that. But now, with the baby, she worries that something bad will happen."

"Something bad? Like what?"

"Oh, anything—that Amanda will get sick, or choke, or that she'll just suddenly stop breathing."

"But, Ekow, Amanda's in perfect health."

He shrugged his shoulders and turned back to his plate, leaving Comfort wondering about Linda's rudeness and her son's unsatisfactory explanation. Had she finally seen a glimpse of Linda's true character? When it rains, she reminded herself, we see that a guinea fowl has five toes.

That night, Comfort lay awake, unable to sleep, listening to Ekow and Linda's voices on the other side of the wall. She couldn't make out what they were saying, but the rhythm and urgency of their tone reminded her of conversations she'd had in her first years of marriage—discussions about money, the children, and most often about her mother-in-law, who'd moved in with them a few months after their wedding.

The old woman had been impossible to please, commanding Comfort on every detail of managing the household, cooking for her husband, and—once the babies arrived—taking care of the children. She complained to Kwaku about any perceived transgressions, and although Comfort tried her best to ignore her mother-in-law's comments, sometimes, when they bit too hard, she complained to Kwaku at night when they were in bed together. Her husband invariably took his mother's side, pointing out that she had suffered for her children, that it was Comfort's duty to respect her husband's mother and turn the other cheek for the sake of maintaining peace in the household. "She's a Fante woman, Comfort, that's her way," he pointed out, adding, "It will be your way, too, someday."

But Comfort had resolved that when she had children of her own she would never cause them the same distress. She'd vowed not to interfere with her daughters-in-law and had, in fact, been able to practice sufficient restraint with her Ghanaian daughters-in-law to forge pleasant relations with them.

Lying in bed, Comfort looked into the darkness of the unfamiliar room, at the looming shapes of the furniture.

She wished once again that her husband were with her, so she could talk to him. In the final years of their marriage, after her mother-in-law had died and the children had left home, their nightly conversations had finally shifted into something new. They had conversed like the closest of friends, with an unexpected level of openness and consideration. It had been a special point in their relationship, one that had taken more than thirty years to build, and it was a cruel irony that those final years had been so brief.

Imagining Kwaku lying next to her at that moment, Comfort could almost evoke his smell, a mix of cigarettes and Lux soap. "I know Ekow is happy I'm here," she whispered to the second pillow that lay beside her, "and Amanda is priceless. But Linda . . . well, it's just as they say about white women—she's complicated. And it's not just what Ekow said about her worrying too much. The problem is I can never tell what she's thinking, and people like that are always full of unpleasant surprises. How can I possibly trust her?"

Comfort shut her eyes, trying to imagine Kwaku's voice answering her. When it finally came to her, his words startled her eyes back open.

"Would it be so hard for you to try to satisfy her, Comfort, for the sake of keeping some peace in this house?"

So clearly did Kwaku's words echo their conversations from the early years of their marriage that Comfort felt a trace of the same shame she'd felt as a young bride when he'd appealed to her to turn the other cheek with his mother.

Maybe she'd pushed Linda too hard tonight. Maybe she'd been meddling, turning into the type of mother-in-law she'd always wanted to avoid becoming. Had her husband been right so long ago—that she would come back to the traditional Fante way, no matter how often she'd resolved not to?

Comfort pulled the covers tightly around her. She would have to learn to keep the peace, to step back and let Linda do things her way when they were together. For her son's sake, for her granddaughter's sake, she could do it. Besides, how hard could it be, since she'd be alone with the baby most of the day?


Within a month, Comfort established a routine that included daily walks with Amanda. She got used to the disposable nappies—and almost felt pride that she never complained to her son that his wife was wasting his money by not using cloth ones. There was a distinct improvement in the shape of Amanda's head, something Comfort never mentioned—not even to her son—despite her satisfaction that the warm compresses and the pillows she carefully arranged around Amanda's head when she napped were taking effect. Both of these things she continued to do in secret and only during the day. Linda had told her more than once never to put any pillows in the baby's crib—one of an ever-growing list of Linda's rules—so they were always safely back on Comfort's bed by the time Linda and Ekow came home.

Overall, Comfort admitted to herself, Linda was not a bad mother; she clearly adored Amanda. But there was always a disquieting urgency in the way she cooed over the baby as soon as she came home, the way she grasped her so close that Amanda sometimes cried out. Soon after her arrival, Linda would retreat to the nursery to breast-feed. Comfort noticed that her daughter-in-law never breast-fed in front of her—as if she hadn't already seen thousands of breasts with suckling babies latched on to them. Meanwhile, Comfort disappeared into the kitchen, pleased to be cooking her son real Ghanaian meals—red *jollof* rice with fish, or spicy palaver sauce made with spinach instead of cocoyam leaves. At the dinner table, Comfort talked mostly with her son, leaving it up to him to bring Linda into their discussions, to navigate the complicated rapids of his wife's moods.

On her daily walks, Comfort began to suspect that her son had been right—the trees were not dead after all. At first, she noticed small brownish balls, like cancerous growths, emerging on the branches of some of the trees, but a week later the growths had burst forth as hundreds and thousands of deep red flowers. Other trees exploded into white blossoms that looked from far away like popped corn. At first Comfort was startled, then enchanted, by the signs of the white man's season of spring. She understood why it was called "spring"—everything seemed to leap forward, to split open. Not just the flowers, but the way people walked about with new energy, were more often outdoors. So much did it raise Comfort's spirits to see Nature rebounding and people milling about that she almost forgot the trepidation she felt around her daughter-in-law. She relished the smell of the earth as it thawed, the cacophony of bird caws and twitters as she pushed her granddaughter's pram to the park.

On a warm, breezy day two months into her stay, Comfort stopped in front of a well-tended garden with an inviting, winding path made of large, flat stones. Her eyes were drawn to a tree, its branches coated with dense pink blossoms. Without thinking, she left Amanda's pram on the sidewalk and stepped up the path toward the tree, until she was startled by a voice behind her. "You like my cherry tree?"

Comfort turned to see an older woman wearing a floppy straw hat and recognized Gerrie. They had seen each other at the park a few more times since their first meeting, each time exchanging pleasantries about the weather and the neighborhood. Had Comfort insulted the closest thing she'd made to a friend by walking onto her property? "I'm sorry," she stammered, "I didn't mean to—"

"No, no, that's fine," Gerrie said. "It's nice to have someone actually notice my garden."

Comfort turned back to the tree and asked Gerrie to repeat its name. From then on, Comfort stopped to talk with her whenever she found her outside. Sometimes, Gerrie put her dog on the leash and accompanied Comfort to the park, pointing out the trees they passed and teaching her their names. When she was alone with Amanda, pushing the pram down the street, Comfort enjoyed silently greeting each tree by its name: the sycamores, with their mottled bark and their branches stretched to make a vast, welcoming shade; the noble Japanese maples, leaves delicate and wine-red; the weeping willow, its branches drooping with the weight of the world.

Comfort also formed a habit of stopping in front of Gerrie's cherry tree every day, whether or not her friend was in her front yard. Even after it shed its blossoms, she'd leave Amanda's pram a few feet away on the sidewalk to touch the gray bark, feeling a familiar yet nameless comfort in the smooth-rough texture against her hand.

On a quiet day halfway into the fourth month of Comfort's visit, Linda unexpectedly returned from work early. She'd complained of not feeling well that morning, and earlier in her stay this might have put Comfort on her guard. But she'd become settled in her routine and had just put Amanda down for her nap, not giving a second thought to the pillows she arranged around the baby's head. It was only when she heard Linda's cry from the bedroom that she jumped up from the couch.

Linda rushed down the stairs clutching Amanda, who'd been startled out of her nap and was crying.

"What are those pillows doing in the crib?" she shouted over the baby's cries. "I've *told* you not to put pillows there."

Comfort was too stunned to censor her words. "You

think I have no wisdom in my head? I've raised six children and eight grandchildren, and not one of them has ever been hurt by a pillow."

"Look, Comfort, maybe people don't know about SIDS in Ghana," Linda answered, the tendons in her neck forming taut lines, "but that's exactly why you need to listen to my instructions."

*Instructions?* Never had she felt so offended, not just at her daughter-in-law's condescending tone but at four months of being treated like a child, as if *she* were the one who needed to be taught how to take care of children. The words came out of her mouth in a breathless rush.

"You think you know everything, but you don't have even the smallest idea of how to take care of a household or a husband, never mind a baby."

Linda tried to interrupt, but Comfort persisted.

"Just because you work in an office doesn't make you smarter than me. I worked in an office, too, before you were even born. But I never let that get in the way of cooking for my husband, and *I* learned to put my feelings aside for the greater peace in the house."

The baby's cries had abated, turning into hiccups. Linda—her face flushed red as if she'd been slapped on both cheeks—stammered, "All I've done since you got here has been to put aside my feelings, to keep my mouth closed when you tell Peter what to do, to force down your greasy food—" She broke off, her face tightening into itself. "If *my* mother were here—"

But she couldn't finish. Her mouth contorted and her eyes narrowed to hold back tears as she turned to rush up the stairs.

In the silent aftermath of their argument, Comfort's heart drummed in her chest. As much to calm herself down as to get away from Linda, she slipped outside and began to walk, her hands still clammy with sweat. It was late in the afternoon and she could keep wandering until Ekow came home—surely he would know how to set things right. Without the pram, her arms felt empty and she wandered aimlessly, trying to lose herself in the now-familiar neighborhood until she found herself on Gerrie's street.

She slowed down her pace as she neared Gerrie's house, scanning the yard for signs of her friend. It was out of the question to share private worries with someone from outside her family, and she would be hard pressed to pretend everything was fine. Satisfied Gerrie wasn't there, she approached the cherry tree and stood in its shade, stroking the tree's trunk, waiting for the sense of calm she usually felt. How could things have gone so terribly awry with Linda? How would they possibly fix what had been said? It would be as hard as mending a broken clay pot to hold water again.

Two children rolled by on their bicycles, laughing. How ridiculous she must look: an old woman standing under a tree, caressing its bark like a lover's skin. She stumbled out from under the shade and continued walking, focusing on the steady rhythm of her shoes against the pavement, the pattern of her breathing.

On the next block, Comfort recognized the familiar lineup of trees along the street. They looked green and lush, so different from the day of her first walk with Amanda, when she'd vowed to stay long enough to see if they came back to life. And she *had* stayed long enough to see the trees change. She'd also stayed long enough to understand that they would soon be transformed again as part of a never-ending cycle, a cycle that paralleled life itself, including her own—her children bearing children, Kwaku's death, and, yes, even someday her own.

A warm breeze wafted by, making the leaves rustle overhead as though they were whispering, reminding her of the passage of time. She looked at her watch. No, she decided, she would not wait for Ekow to come home. Not that she looked forward to the conversation she would have to have with Linda, but she had certainly survived much worse. She would have to choose her words more carefully than her mother-in-law had, but whatever words she picked, and whichever ones Linda used to answer, in the end they would be nothing more than a ripple in the span of her life, a puff of air passing through a tree's leaves.

# The Civilized World

The morning of their departure from the Dzanga-Sangha Park, Janice and Bruce woke up early so they would be ready when the driver came to pick them up for the long trip back to Bangui. From the veranda of the guesthouse, they watched the burnt orange sun rise over the Sangha River, the smooth motions of the fishermen rowing their pirogues upstream. In the distance, Janice heard the muted cries of birds, as if they, too, were waking up, stretching their vocal cords just as Bruce was now stretching his lanky arms.

Janice felt the heat in her hand from the enameled mug she brought to her lips, tasting the sugary tea with condensed milk—Bruce, who was British, referred to coffee as *vile*. She watched him dip a small, stale beignet into his tea before stuffing it into his mouth. After he wiped his hand on his shorts, he shifted his long legs in the wooden armchair and began tapping his fingernails against his cup.

Despite the serene surroundings, Janice could tell Bruce

was on edge. Throughout their two weeks in the Central African Republic, in fact, he'd been pensive and jittery. She could guess why, too. He'd been working in the international development business only a few years, and his two years in Senegal, where they were both currently posted, had hardly prepared him for a country like this. She, on the other hand, had lived in Africa for the last fifteen years, managing projects that were supposed to—and rarely did—make a dent in the health status of the population. Her career had started here in the C.A.R., where she'd spent three years as a Peace Corps Volunteer, and on this trip she had found things to be pretty much as she'd expected. After more than a dozen years of civil unrest, everything was slightly worse.

Before coming to the Dzanga-Sangha Park, they'd stayed with her former colleague in Bangui—now a professor at the university—who lived in a house without running water, the only sign of electricity a single fluorescent light affixed to the outside wall of his house. Bruce, with his clear ideas of right and wrong, was bothered by the fact that so many people had so little in a country blessed with abundant natural resources.

"Penny for your thoughts," she said, then added an attempt at levity. "Make that five CFA."

Bruce sipped his tea and looked at her over the rim of his cup without smiling. "I was thinking about those poor pygmy ladies, actually."

Janice tried to ignore his use of the term *pygmy*, which she'd already told him—after they went on a tour of the rain forest with three of the women—was considered derogatory. Well over a foot shorter than Janice, who'd always considered herself barely average in height, the women had navigated them effortlessly through the dark forest, pointing out medicinal plants along the way. When they smiled, they flashed rows of teeth filed down to sharp points. Two wore *pagne* cloths wrapped around their bodies and knotted at their chests; the third one had tied hers around her waist, leaving her elongated breasts bare, their two pointed shapes forming a *W* across her chest.

"What *about* the Baka women?" Janice asked, hoping he'd pick up on her use of their ethnic name.

"I was just wondering why the park staff doesn't do more to help them."

It was a typical comment coming from a do-gooder like Bruce. After all, he worked for an organization that supported the orphaned and handicapped children of Dakar. This was a man who thought he could solve all of Africa's problems by handing out money.

But Janice knew the people who ran the park; she knew they cared about the Baka. "They *do* help them, Bruce. They give them jobs, and they're protecting the forest around them from being decimated so they can keep on living there."

"But look at their living conditions—they go about practically starkers; they use plants as medicine. At the very least, the park should build them a proper hospital."

Janice felt herself begin to bristle at his self-righteousness. "This is their culture, Bruce. Why make them live like us?"

"I'm not saying *make* them do anything, Janice. If they had a choice to live with the same creature comforts we enjoy, they'd surely do it."

"And leave all of this"—Janice swept her arm across the view of the river—"for the rat race of the civilized world?" She fought the temptation to wiggle her fingers in the air to mimic quotation marks around her last two words. What did it mean to be civilized, anyway? It couldn't just mean skyscrapers and cell phones and cars. From what she understood, Africa held the oldest civilizations on earth. "How do you know whether their quality of life is better or worse than ours?"

"Bollocks!" he said. "Do you have any idea what their life expectancy is?"

Janice shook her head. "No, I don't. I suspect it's at least as low as the rest of the country, though, somewhere in the mid-forties."

"Precisely. So you'd rather they clung to their culture, at the cost of living lives that are shorter than ours by half, just so you can fantasize about them having some mythical, carefree existence?"

He had backed her into a corner. Of course the Central Africans—the Baka and all the others, regardless of their ethnic group—were entitled to the same standard of living as anyone else. She just couldn't stomach the way he dismissed their culture—which he knew nothing about—as if it didn't matter, as if everything about it was bad. He should at least listen to her viewpoint, at least acknowledge that the world wasn't as sharply delineated by his right and everyone else's wrong. "All I'm saying is their culture deserves—"

But he cut her off with a wave of his hand. "Oh, stop talking out your arse, Janice."

His tone was light, bordering on teasing, but the dismissive wave of his hand—as if he were batting away an insect—made her cheeks tingle as the blood rose to her head. At the sound of a motor in the distance, she felt a surge of relief. Their driver, Dicudonné, would be there in a moment in their rented Land Cruiser. She retreated inside to throw her toothbrush and flip-flops into her bag. As she closed the zipper and tried to collect herself, to adjust her breathing to its regular rhythm, she couldn't help wonder once again if Bruce was really the man she wanted to be the father of her children someday.

It would be a long trip for two people not to talk with each other, fourteen hours if everything went well and the Land Cruiser didn't get stuck somewhere along the pockmarked dirt road. Sitting in the front seat next to Dieudonné, with Bruce behind them, Janice watched the rusty-colored ribbon of road ahead. So far they hadn't seen a single other vehicle; it was perfectly conceivable that they wouldn't until they reached M'Baïki. At first she enjoyed the silence—let him stew in his cultural superiority for a while; let him realize his insensitivity had hurt her feelings. His gaffes and arrogant attitude had been a source of embarrassment

throughout their trip—like when he'd expressed his aston-
ishment to their host in Bangui that a university professor
lived without modern amenities. Two days ago, he'd offended
Dieudonné, too, by lecturing him for having six children.
She wondered if Bruce had even noticed that since then the
driver stopped talking to him, no longer using his French or
his smattering of English and only addressing Janice—
always in Sango.

In the past when they'd had similar disagreements
about development taking precedence over culture, she'd
been able to let it go by reminding herself that he'd spent
much less time in Africa than she had. Surely he would
eventually come around to appreciate the continent's com-
plexity, and then—she imagined it being like a snake molt-
ing its useless old skin—he would shed his self-righteousness.
He might finally disassociate himself from the tiring, smug
Westerners who thought Africa needed to follow in their
footsteps—that capitalism and democracy were the only
way to go. He, too, would admire the way African culture
revered old people rather than discarding them, the way it
valued human relationships over material goods. Traditional culture, at least—much of it had been destroyed by
urbanization. She'd experienced that firsthand two years
ago when her house in Abidjan was broken into by two
armed robbers in the middle of the night.

Better not to dwell on that, Janice reminded herself. She
was on vacation, after all. A pair of white butterflies fluttered
past her window, two flecks of white that flashed by so

quickly she wondered if she'd imagined them. In their wake she saw nothing but an endless swath of green forest sweeping past on either side of the road. She looked over at Dieudonné's profile, his eyes narrowed into slits as he focused on the road ahead. The almond shape of his eyes made Janice wonder if he was Yakoma, but she decided against asking. When she'd lived in the C.A.R., ethnic identities weren't a big deal, but she knew that things had changed. After her Peace Corps service ended, she'd followed the stories of Yakomas being targeted by government forces.

"Dieudonné, what village are you from?" she asked.

"I was born in Mobaye," he answered, without taking his eyes off the road. "But I grew up in Bangui."

Janice nodded. A southerner. Maybe Yakoma, possibly Sango. "You're a *Banguisois*, then."

This time, he glanced over at her. "For now," he said, "but I don't plan to grow old there. When I die, I'll be buried in my village."

Janice nodded, more to herself than to Dieudonné. It wasn't the first time she'd heard an African speak frankly about his own death or express sentiments about returning home when his time came. What did it feel like to have such a strong sense of home, a bond to place as strong as an umbilical cord? She felt no similar urge to return to the United States. If anything, Africa had come to feel more like home to her, even though she knew rationally she'd always be an outsider. Of course, Rena, her therapist back in Dakar, blamed Janice's sense of displacement on her childhood, on

the fact that her family had moved every year or two for her
father's peripatetic military career.


No matter how hard Janice tried to explain, Rena didn't
seem to understand how she could refer to the armed robbery in Abidjan as a gift. Though her sleep was regularly
hampered by nightmares of being buried alive, during her
waking hours Janice recognized that her ordeal had served
to bring her life into crystal-clear focus. She was lucky to
be alive.

The robbers hadn't physically harmed her; instead, they'd
locked her into one of her closets, and anything that happened after she was liberated was preferable to being confined
for eighteen hours in a dark and musty coffinlike space,
initially terrified the assailants would return and then fight-
ing a mounting sense of panic that no one would find her.
The material things they'd stolen were inconsequential, and
none of the problems that used to frustrate her at the
office—the Minister of Health canceling a meeting, the project car breaking down, an employee quitting—seemed worth
getting worked up over anymore; none of them paralleled
having to pee in the corner of her closet while she waited to be
rescued. What *had* become important, what had suddenly
snapped into focus after years of pouring all her energy into
her work, was that at thirty-nine years old she wanted to have
children, a longing that injected a new urgency into her
previously lukewarm efforts to find a mate.

Janice started seeing Rena soon after she relocated to Dakar, a move prompted by her headquarters. A few months after the robbery, when she'd missed several reporting deadlines and after what the Human Resources Department termed a "downturn in performance," they'd strongly suggested a transfer to Dakar and therapy with Rena. The term "posttraumatic stress disorder" had been bandied about with sympathy. They were magnanimous, offering a year's paid therapy—up to two, if Rena deemed she needed it. Janice wondered if the lawyers at headquarters feared she might bring a lawsuit against her company for not having done enough to protect her—an absurd notion, of course. In the meantime, the political situation in Abidjan had grown increasingly volatile anyway, so she accepted the transfer and its condition.

Like a dentist checking each of her teeth for signs of decay, Rena meticulously probed Janice's feelings around the break-in. Did Janice feel betrayed by her house guard, whose voice she'd recognized as one of the two robbers? Wasn't she angry that the police had never tracked either of them down before she left? Was she now afraid of living alone? Did she find herself being more suspicious than before of African men?

Janice jumped on that one. "Two bad apples don't mean the whole barrel's rotten."

Rena seemed to contemplate this before she continued, tugging absentmindedly at a strand of red hair that sprang back to its natural curly shape when she let go. "You know,

Janice, sometimes people with PTSD don't want to accept what's happening to them—"

"I'm not in denial," Janice said, not for the first time.

"But the nightmares. . . ."

"I hardly have them anymore," Janice lied, forcing Rena to move on, to poke at other areas of her psyche—her childhood and past loves.

When Janice met Bruce a year into her stint in Senegal, she finally had something seemingly innocuous to talk about with Rena. At first she didn't think it would go anywhere—he wasn't really her type, so lanky and pale—until she realized that Bruce was as ready to settle down as she was, that he, too, wanted children. From there, things progressed so quickly that it almost felt like she had no choice in the matter, as if some force or energy were shooting them forward like a car barreling downhill without brakes. But she knew she'd had a choice when he asked her to marry him five months after they met—she'd been the one to say yes.

Rena had once told her that a couple's differences weren't as important as how they dealt with those differences. How would it ever work if Bruce couldn't even listen to, much less respect, what Janice was trying to say? Three hours into the drive she was ready to talk to him if he made the first move, but it was unlikely based on his continued silence. If she wanted them to work out some kind of understanding— even if it was just to agree to disagree—she would probably have to be the one to take the first step.

Outside her window, Janice noticed another white

butterfly, then two more, floating past them randomly like shreds of paper blowing in the wind. Within minutes, there were hundreds of them, fluttering around the car like a tropical snowstorm, tumbling against the front windshield, floating beside the side windows in a thick and hypnotic freefall. As Dieudonné turned on the windshield wipers, Janice was reminded of the blizzards in the years her family had lived in the northern parts of the United States. She decided that butterflies made as good a peace offering as any.

Without turning around in her seat, she asked Bruce, "Don't the butterflies remind you of snow?"

When he didn't answer, she finally turned around.

He was asleep, had probably been asleep all the time she'd been stewing over their argument, running her mind along the sharp edges of their differences of opinion. Somehow, Bruce had mastered the African skill of sleeping in cars, no matter how bumpy the ride. His head dangled backward over his seat, his mouth open like a baby bird. It hurt Janice's neck just to look at him, so she turned around again, a hot surge in her chest as she watched the windshield wipers smearing crushed butterflies across the window. How dare he sleep, carefree, after he'd wounded her with his words? How could he be so inconsiderate?

Without warning, the car lurched—almost as if it had the hiccups—and then stalled. At the sight of the continuing flurry of butterflies outside her window, Janice had the sensation of being inside a snow globe, only in reverse, with the white flecks outside. She pictured a gigantic hand reaching down and shaking their car; maybe that would get it to start again.

Dieudonné pushed open his door, climbed down, and propped open the hood.

Without air-conditioning, the air inside the car began to heat up. In the backseat, Bruce's head had shifted sideways, his face squashed against the window. Still, he was fast asleep. She could shout at him or poke him awake. No, she decided, let him slowly bake.

She stepped out and joined Dieudonné to ask him what was wrong.

"*Apapalapo ti la*," he answered. Though she'd begun to remember long-forgotten Sango words over the last two weeks, she had to ask him to repeat what he'd said. Instead, he pointed in the air and then at the car, and she finally understood that the butterflies had clogged something in the motor.

She watched as Dieudonné picked up a stick from the side of the road and began to poke it through the grille, a tendon in his upper arm tensing as he flicked off the dead butterflies, their torn and broken wings littering the ground at his feet like white confetti.

She'd originally planned to travel solo to the C.A.R., a trip to visit friends she hadn't seen in twelve years. When Bruce proposed to her a month before she was due to leave, they'd decided he would come along. She'd already agreed to marry him, of course, but there was a part of her that recalled the age-old advice that there was no better way to figure out if you were compatible with someone than to travel with them to a remote location—and the C.A.R. certainly fit the qualifier of *remote*.

When she'd hinted to Rena that this trip might be a litmus test, Rena had stared at her for several seconds. "He works for a group that supports orphans, Janice. He sounds like a great guy." Was Janice imagining it or was Rena talking slower than usual, like a grade-school teacher spelling something out to her student?

"If you're serious about wanting a family," Rena continued, "you'll have to accept that there's no such thing as a perfect relationship or a perfect man."

Janice thought of Rena's husband, whom she'd met by the Sofitel pool on a recent Saturday: a squat, balding man who worked for the State Department and had complained loudly about the poolside service. Rena had certainly followed her own advice.

Still, she was wrong about Janice's fear of commitment. Maybe when she'd been younger she'd been carefree and a bit restless, but that had all changed after eighteen hours of solitary confinement in her closet. She knew what she wanted now.

Behind her, Janice heard the car door open and slam shut.

"It's a bloody oven in there," Bruce said, waving his arm to shoo away the butterflies. "Why did we stop?"

"It's the butterflies," she told him, relieved that they were talking again. "They seem to have clogged up something in the motor."

"The butterflies?"

She nodded.

He burst out laughing, but Janice didn't share his amusement. Instead, her earlier relief was replaced by resentment. Didn't he realize how much he'd offended her? Had he honestly forgotten their argument, or was he just pretending it never happened?

"That's just brilliant," he said, still chuckling. "What's next, I wonder, termites chewing up the tires?"

She decided not to point out that termites ate wood, not rubber, and pointedly looked away into the forest. She could feel him watching her, contemplating her before he said, "In a bit of a mood, are we?"

She ignored his question and walked to the side of the road, where she squatted down on her haunches, assuming the waiting position she'd learned from using public transportation on countless African road trips. Bruce muttered something about going to the loo, and she watched him walk down the side of the road toward the edge of the forest. When it came to relieving himself, Bruce's habits were decidedly un-African. Even with his biological advantage he approached bathroom breaks with more modesty than she did.

At the sight of Bruce retreating through the flurry of white butterflies, a long-forgotten picture rose in Janice's mind: her father walking off into thickly falling snow. Christmas 1972. He had come home from Vietnam for the holidays, and Janice, eleven years old at the time, had helped her mother for weeks to prepare for his return, decorating the house, baking cookies, even shopping for her outfit to greet him at the airport.

The day of his arrival, her sister Clara, who was five years older than Janice and hadn't participated in any of the preparations, refused to go to the airport. She spent two full days at her boyfriend's house, only coming home at nightfall, until Christmas Day, when her mother insisted she stay home—a huge mistake that resulted in Clara calling her father a baby killer, their mother sending Clara to her room, and her father grabbing his coat and storming off into the snowy outdoors in the direction of the woods behind their house.

Janice chased after him, calling out for him to slow down so she could catch up, but he kept on walking. She tried to step in his footprints in the deep snow that reached her knees, but the space between his prints was too far for her short legs and she had to push her way through the snow, her pant legs getting icy wet. When she finally caught up with him, her heart thumping against her chest and her breath escaping from her mouth in puffs, she was panting too hard to say any of the things she wanted to say—to tell him that her sister was wrong, to let him know she loved him.

"Why are you following me?" her father asked, his voice loud and angry.

Too winded to answer, Janice reached out to touch his

arm, but he pulled away and told her to go home. Then he turned and continued his long-legged march into the woods.

Even now, three decades later and far away in a different country, Janice could recall the sting of rejection, how it hurt even more than the pain from her freezing toes and ears or the bite of the wind blowing against the icy tears on her bare face. How could he have been so callous? She felt a flash of anger, the blood rising to her head as it had that morning. She would never treat her child that way, never. Nor would Bruce, she had to admit. She'd watched him with the orphans, how he let the courageous ones touch his white skin to see if it felt different from their own, how he coaxed the shy ones to play. In Bangui, where many of the children she'd known back then were grown up with kids of their own, babies had been shoved into their arms like warm bread loaves. The image of Bruce holding one of them in his arms had been the single reminder during this trip of why she'd agreed to marry him, the one thing that made the decision still feel okay.

Rena was right—Bruce didn't need to be perfect— especially when she was so far from perfect herself. At least she had to give him credit for having joined her on this trip; it couldn't be easy for him to be here, not speaking the language and not knowing anyone but her.

Janice stood up and walked to the edge of the forest where Bruce had disappeared. Other than a few clanging noises from Dieudonné's direction, she heard nothing but silence as the butterflies continued to drift in the air. Remembering how quickly she'd lost her sense of direction in the forest with the Baka women, Janice began to worry. Maybe Bruce had wandered too far. What if he couldn't find his way back?

Behind her, she heard a rustle of leaves and spun around. Bruce stepped out of the forest just a few feet away, wiping his hands on his pants as he approached her.

"Looking for me?" he asked.

In her relief, the corners of her mouth began to lift into a smile of forgiveness, but before she could answer him, Dieudonné's voice called out, "*A leke awe.*" He was already climbing up into the driver's seat. "*E gwe ma,*" he shouted.

"What did he say?" Bruce asked.

"He said it's fixed. We can go now."

"Well, that's a relief," he said.

As they walked toward the car, side by side, Dieudonné tried starting it, the motor turning several times before it stalled again. They stopped in their tracks.

"*A leke awe ape,*" Janice corrected him jokingly, as Dieudonné stepped back down again and headed to the motor. He flashed her a smile and held his arms out, palms up, as if to say, *I'm doing what I can with these hands, but it's really in the hands of a higher power*, a litany Janice had heard plenty of times before.

Janice turned back to Bruce and saw that he had been watching her interaction with Dieudonné. He gave a little snort. "He's not the brightest chap, now, is he?" he said, not even bothering to lower his voice in case Dieudonné could hear. As Janice stared at him, drop-jawed, he added, "Maybe if he spent less time siring children and more time learning about cars, we'd be on our merry way by now."

She felt her body grow rigid with anger. How dare he speak like this? Who was he to pass judgment on another being? She grappled for the words to strip him of his arrogance, to make him see how wrong he was. But what was the point? His outburst had confirmed what she'd known all along. Other than their shared desire for children, they were as incongruous as a snowstorm in tropical sunshine.

Bruce was watching her, his head tilted to the side. "What's wrong now?"

She almost laughed at his use of the word *now*, suggesting that she was the problem, that she was once again *in a bit of a mood*. They would have to talk eventually, of course. But this was neither the time nor the place, not just because Dieudonné understood enough English to make out what they said but because, despite everything, Bruce had taken this trip for her. Better to break it off once they were both back in familiar territory.

"Nothing," she finally said, turning away. "Nothing that can't wait."

She could already imagine the confusion and awkwardness in Dakar among their friends, who'd be forced to split into two camps. She could picture Rena absorbing the news of her breakup with Bruce, imperceptibly shaking her head as if Janice would never find someone now, would never have the family she craved. But she didn't care. She only had to see Rena for a few more months before her two years were up, and there were other ways to have babies than the old-fashioned way. Why not adopt on her own? And maybe, if she was lucky, the right man would still materialize—not a compromise, not a desperate choice, but a conscious, discerning one.

Behind her, Janice heard the sound of a car door slamming, the ignition turning. This time, the motor caught, turned smoothly, and continued to run without stalling. Dieudonné jumped down from the driver's seat and lowered the hood with a loud clatter. Bruce had already begun to stride toward the Land Cruiser, walking with long-legged, purposeful steps through the flurry of butterflies, not bothering to turn around and check if she was following him.

# The Precious Brother Salon

The day the Precious Brother Salon opened for business, Adjoa stood on the threshold, scanning the newly polished floor and the pristine white walls that smelled of fresh paint. A pair of dryer hoods and hair-washing stations stood along the right wall, across from four black swivel chairs, each with its own round mirror. At the far end of the room, she'd set up a manicure table and, across from the front desk, two stuffed chairs she hoped would feel welcoming to her clients.

The salon looked just as she'd pictured it when she and her twin brother, Kojo, lived in the Ivory Coast for almost thirteen years, saving money to start their own business upon their return to Ghana. Still, it was hard to relish this moment, to take any measure of pride in the realization of their joint dream. Instead, Adjoa felt something akin to motion sickness. She entered the room and began pacing, touching the back of one of the swivel chairs and spinning it around full circle. Was this normal anxiety over opening a business, she wondered, or was it because of her family's ultimatum that her venture must make a profit within six months?

Adjoa reached up to touch her hair, felt the bun at the nape of her neck, and patted down a few stray hairs. It was a gesture Kojo had often made fun of, the way she tried to keep every hair in place, in what her twin brother referred to as her "God-fearing" look.

At the thought of Kojo, Adjoa felt a dull familiar throb in her right arm. Here it came again, the same pain that had started right after his death. The doctors she'd consulted were mystified, subjecting her to tests and X-rays that proved useless to explain its cause. She stopped consulting the experts when her childhood friend Gifty, in the course of a conversation about Gifty's work as a nurse, happened to mention phantom pain: the sensations that amputees feel in their lost limbs for years following an amputation. Losing her twin—with whom she'd shared everything, even her mother's womb—had been even more agonizing than the loss of a limb. Although more than a year had passed since she'd buried Kojo in Abidjan and traveled back to Accra, telling her family that he'd died of cerebral malaria, Adjoa had begun to think of the on-again, off-again ache as a form of phantom pain.

With time, she'd learned to live with it. Much harder to bear was her guilt over the lie she'd told her family—a lie that created a gulf that was further widened by their disagreement over Adjoa and Kojo's savings. How ironic that when she lived in Abidjan she'd called them every week, and now that she lived in the same city she saw them as rarely as she could.

"Madam?"

Adjoa spun around. Yaa, the assistant she'd hired the previous week, stood in the doorway, sensibly dressed in a skirt and short-sleeved blouse.

"Come in, come in," Adjoa said. "I'm glad to see you're so prompt, Yaa."

"Yes, madam," she answered, as she stepped inside.

"I think I'd prefer you to call me Adjoa."

Yaa nodded. "I noticed the new sign outside," she said. "Surely your brother will be pleased to be recognized."

"The sign maker put it up yesterday," Adjoa explained, ignoring the second half of Yaa's comment—after all, she knew nothing about her family or Adjoa's loss. "I think he did a fine job."

The sign maker, as it turned out, had been a lazy and possibly dishonest man, coming up with excuses why he needed more time to complete the job, and even asking for more money weeks after they'd agreed on the price. She'd finally asked her eldest brother, Kobby, to call the man and bully him into bringing the sign—just the type of complication Kojo would have stepped in to fix had he been alive. "You haven't even opened the business and already you're running across problems," Kobby said, prompting Adjoa to vow never again to ask him for help. Somehow she would just have to manage on her own.

But once the sign—its letters painted in graceful blue cursive—was delivered and affixed, she immediately forgot about the annoyances she'd had with the sign maker. She was particularly pleased by her decision to add the Nkon- sonkonson Adinkra symbol, signifying "we are linked in both life and death." As for the name, it had come to her one day when she looked at the rear bumper of a *tro-tro* bus on Tetteh Quarshie roundabout. The driver had painted an Akan expression, a public display of his gratitude for his brother's financial support for the bus: A GOOD BROTHER IS PRECIOUS.

As if she had already been working there for weeks, Yaa approached the shelf above the washing station and pulled down one of the folded candy-pink smocks stacked there. She shook it out and pushed her arms through the sleeves. "Shall I make you a cup of tea?" she asked.

Adjoa smiled. She'd made a good choice in hiring Yaa, a recent graduate from the same beauty school Adjoa had attended years ago. In fact, the girl reminded her a bit of herself at a young age. She'd also hired two teenage girls as apprentices, but her hopes for them were much more mod- est. They were awfully young and would need to be super- vised closely—even to make sure they came to work on time, Adjoa thought, as she checked her watch and noted it was already past their official opening time of seven o'clock.

"Yes, please, Yaa, make us both some tea, please. And

when the apprentices come, be sure to instruct them that making tea will be one of their responsibilities."

While Yaa went into the back room—a large closet, really—to heat the water on the hotplate, Adjoa looked down at the appointment book splayed open on the counter before her. The week's schedule consisted of vast blocks of white with only a smattering of names, a few clients from her previous job at a different salon. For today, she'd written down the name of a single client: her friend Gifty.

Adjoa had invested all of her and Kojo's savings into the salon—with nothing left over to pay the first month's bills—and only one client was scheduled to come in the first day. She rubbed her right arm, trying to massage away the ache. Could this possibly be typical for the first day of a new salon?

Kobby was right: she knew nothing about running a business.

Her family had objected to her plans from the beginning. After distributing Kojo's clothes at the forty-day celebration of his death, they'd refused to grant her permission to use the money she and Kojo had saved in Abidjan. The family felt it belonged to all of them, even though it came primarily from Adjoa's own earnings. When she tried to explain that Kojo would have wanted her to open the salon, her words seemed to leave no more of an impression than a fly buzzing past an elephant.

Even though technically the money was in her name, Adjoa wouldn't use it without her family's blessing. When her friend Gifty suggested she could hire a lawyer to settle the problem, Adjoa recoiled at the thought. This was a family matter. Why bring in someone from the outside? Not wanting to touch the savings until they'd reached an agreement, she found work as a hairdresser at a large salon to pay her living expenses. But the job only confirmed what she already knew: although she liked to interact with the customers, she hated having a boss who treated her like a disposable worker, acting as if she were being benevolent when she paid Adjoa's salary.

The only thing Adjoa knew for sure about running a business was that she wanted to run hers differently from all the places she'd worked in the past. She wanted her salon to be the cleanest, friendliest, and most welcoming in the city—no, in the whole country.

At the one-year anniversary celebration of Kojo's death, her brother Kobby, who represented the family since neither parent was still alive, had finally announced that she could proceed with her plans for the salon, with a caveat. "It's best for all of us," Kobby explained to the congregated family, "if the money is put into a solid investment so that Adjoa can help out in difficult times."

Then he turned to Adjoa.

"But you need to prove the salon is a good investment. You'll need to show us you can run a business. If in six months it begins to earn a profit, we'll drop the matter. Otherwise, we sell the business and find a better investment."

The two apprentices arrived at the Precious Brother Salon at the same time, bounding in with the unfettered energy of young puppies. Adjoa had hired them separately, and only now noticed how similar they looked: equally short, with newly formed breasts straining at their blouses, faces round with baby fat, and their hair braided in the same style along their scalps. This was further complicated by the fact that they both went by highly similar Christian names, Suzie and Sylvia, instead of their traditional ones. Adjoa would have to make every effort not to confuse them and accidentally call one of them by the wrong name.

Yaa handed the girls their smocks and took them to the back room to show them the tea cupboard and cleaning utensils. Adjoa sipped her warm tea, the satisfying taste of sweetened condensed milk lingering on her tongue as her friend Gifty walked into the salon accompanied by a generously proportioned older woman with a scarf wrapped around her head like a crown.

"*Akwaaba*," Adjoa said to both women. "You are welcome."

Gifty handed her a small brass bell and explained it was meant to be hung from the front door to announce visitors, so that Adjoa could properly welcome them.

"How thoughtful of you," Adjoa said, as she clasped her friend's small frame against hers.

Gifty introduced the older woman as her Auntie Comfort, and Adjoa called for one of the apprentices to bring tea for the women.

"*Akwaaba*," she repeated again, motioning at the chairs. "Please have a seat."

Gifty settled down in one of the chairs while the older woman meandered around the salon as if she were an inspector rather than a customer.

"I'm sorry," Gifty whispered to Adjoa, as her auntie paused to examine the ceiling. "She's a bit choosy, and she's never found a salon she's willing to go to twice. She needs a wash and set, and my cousin ran out of places to take her, so I offered to bring her along."

Adjoa nodded, kneading her right arm with the left.

"Your arm is still bothering you?" Gifty asked.

"I'm sure it will be fine," Adjoa said, dropping her arm. "And we'll do our best to please your auntie."

By the time Suzie—or Sylvia—had placed a tray with two cups of tea and a plate of digestive biscuits on the small table between the easy chairs, Comfort had circled the salon and announced, "Well, it seems clean enough."

Not sure if the comment was directed at Gifty or at herself, Adjoa took the opportunity to say thank you. She beckoned to Yaa and introduced her to the two women.

"Yaa will wash your hair, Gifty, while I take care of Auntie."

She ushered Comfort to one of the swivel chairs, where she untied the head scarf to reveal a flattened mass of permed hair. She began gently to comb it out.

"I smell paint," Comfort said. "How long has your salon been open?"

"This is our first week, Auntie," Adjoa answered. "Our first day, in fact."

"And where did you train?"

"At the beauty school on Labadi Road," she said, wondering how the staff in all the other salons—the ones where Gifty said Comfort no longer went—had taken to Comfort's probing questions. "And I worked at a hotel salon in Abidjan for many years."

Comfort looked up. "You've lived in the Ivory Coast?"

"That's right, Auntie."

From across the room, Gifty spoke up. "Don't try to ask her about her time there, Auntie. She won't even talk to me about it."

"Well, it's not so important to talk about as it is to have experienced it," Comfort said, with a definitive nod of her head. "I've told all my children it's important to see the world beyond our borders—if only to appreciate coming home again. But of my six children, only one son has gone abroad, to America. I'm sure Gifty already told you that I visited him there."

"No, she hadn't mentioned it."

Comfort took a sip from her tea and continued as if she hadn't heard Adjoa. "It's a beautiful country—you can't imagine until you see it for yourself. I would have stayed longer than four months except I had to return to prepare for the one-year anniversary of my husband's passing."

Adjoa merely nodded, trying to concentrate on loosening a knot in the older woman's hair. Kojo's one-year anniversary had taken place five months ago, and after Kobby officially offered the family's compromise, he'd sat her down for a private conversation.

"Some members of the family," he said, "are still upset that you didn't bring back Kojo's body to be buried in his own country. As for me, it just doesn't make sense."

Adjoa listened, her head bowed.

"We don't blame you for his death, Adjoa. It's not your fault the malaria killed him; it was just his time. But how could you bury him in a foreign country, where his soul will forever wander and not find rest? Have you forgotten your culture? Have you forgotten the hands that fed and nurtured you?"

"No, Kobby," Adjoa said. "I haven't forgotten. But I know it's what Kojo would have wanted. I wish you would understand."

Kobby shook his head thoughtfully. "Something doesn't make sense, Adjoa. You and Kojo were like two halves of a pod. Yes, you both had plans for the money when he was alive, but it doesn't make sense for you to choose those plans over providing him a peaceful final resting place."

"Adjoa?" Comfort's tone was sharp. How many times had she called her name before Adjoa heard her?

"Yes, Auntie," she said, trying to keep her tone light and conversational.

"Where has your head wandered off to? I asked you what style you recommend for my hair."

Adjoa put aside the comb and patted Comfort's hair for

several moments. "A simple set, I think, with an inward curl. Though you might also like me to trim the ends."

Comfort nodded. "Just a trim, though, not too much. Your head is someplace else this morning. If I don't look at what you're doing, you'll give me the wrong haircut."


Later that morning, the Precious Brother Salon received its third client, a young woman who came on foot rather than by car, poking her head in the door like a frightened bird.

"I don't have an appointment," she said, her hands fluttering around her neck, clasping and unclasping themselves. Her hair was unpermed, stray strands escaping from the braided rows along her scalp.

While Adjoa stepped out from behind the counter and assured her that not having an appointment was quite all right, Comfort looked up from her seat in one of the easy chairs, a fresh cup of tea at her side and an opened magazine in her lap. Adjoa had already finished Comfort's hair, but Yaa was still tending to Gifty, whose hair was being dressed into an elaborate design of twists and curls.

After Adjoa asked one of the apprentices—she thought it was Suzie—to bring another cup of tea, she turned to the newcomer and said, "I'm Adjoa, and you are . . . ?"

The girl—for that was what she seemed to Adjoa—had perked up at the suggestion of tea. "I'm Gladys."

Motioning for her to sit down, Adjoa asked, "And what can we do for you today, Gladys?"

"What can you . . . ?" She seemed confused, her hands becoming restless again as she sat down on the chair next to Comfort.

"Your hair," said Comfort. "You're in a salon, after all."

"Oh, yes, of course." Gladys's hand flew to the collar of her blouse, flipping it up and down as she continued. "Well, I'm not sure. My boyfriend says I should do something fashionable, but I can't decide between a perm or curls."

Adjoa tried to ignore the agitated movements of the girl's hands, which were distracting and made her want to massage her sore right arm. "It depends on how much time you have to take care of your hair," she told Gladys. "With a perm you have to come back to have it washed and reset every week. A better option might be curls—all you have to do is put activator on every morning, comb it out, and you're ready to go."

Gladys nodded, then asked in a low voice, "How much do you charge for curls?"

"Forty thousand cedis," Adjoa said. "Twenty thousand if you bring your own kit. Would you like more time to think about it?"

"No," Gladys said, straightening her back, her hands finally still in her lap. "I want curls. I'll go to the market for the kit and come back this afternoon."

After Gladys left, Comfort made a sound as if she were clearing her throat. Had Adjoa done something to displease her? She turned around and found the older woman smiling.

"Most hairdressers would have pushed a perm on that impressionable girl," Comfort said, "just so she would have to come back every week to spend more money."

Since there didn't seem to be a need to respond—her words had come out as a statement, not a question—Adjoa merely shrugged.

"How much do you know about running a business?" the older woman asked, closing the magazine and settling her behind more comfortably in the chair.

Adjoa felt herself bristle. "I know enough."

"Enough to know that child probably can't afford to come here every week anyway, but that she might refer her friends if she leaves here pleased?"

Despite Comfort's meddling, Adjoa couldn't help liking her. Moreover, she'd begun to form a suspicion, despite Comfort's brusque manner, that the feeling was mutual. "I hadn't thought of it that way, Auntie. I just want my clients to leave here satisfied."

Comfort nodded her head. "My son that I told you about—the one who lives in America—he sells cars, and he always says satisfied clients bring more clients."

Adjoa sighed. "He may be right, but with just three clients on my first day, I do wish I had more of a plan."

"You already have one, my dear," Comfort informed her. "You just said it yourself—customer satisfaction. I have no doubt your salon will do quite well."

Adjoa stared at Comfort sitting perched in her chair, an aura of unquestionable authority around her. Her words felt like a blessing, a much-needed rainfall on the parched earth after a prolonged dry season. Like the market vendors' superstition that the first customer of the morning sets the tone for the rest of their day's business, she hoped Comfort's words were a good omen for her salon's future.

But before Adjoa could thank Comfort for her encouragement, Gifty had joined them, her hair twisted in rows across her scalp, a fountain of false curls cascading down the back of her head. The sides of Comfort's mouth lifted slightly, but she said nothing.

"Yaa did a fantastic job," said Gifty, her face radiant as she settled the bill. "Thank you, Adjoa. I'll be sure to send my friends here."

Adjoa looked up in time to catch Comfort's piercing, I-told-you-so look.

Despite Comfort's blessing, clients only trickled in for the first several weeks after the salon opened. Still, Adjoa made sure that Yaa and the apprentices greeted every customer and offered them tea and biscuits before a hair on their head was touched. When Suzie and Sylvia weren't busy, she had them sit outside on a bench to welcome clients as soon as they stepped out of their cars and offer to help carry any bags inside. If Adjoa noticed that a client was visibly hungry, she sent one of the apprentices to a nearby chop bar to bring back a steaming plate of *redred*, refusing to let the client pay her back. She made sure that the salon stayed as spotless as it had been on the very first day.

Adjoa also did her best not to be like her previous bosses and take the salon staff for granted. When she left the shop for errands, she put Yaa in charge, letting her know that she trusted her. Once she discovered that Suzie had a gap between her two front teeth, she was able to distinguish between the apprentices and always made sure to call them by name. Under Adjoa and Yaa's tutelage, the apprentices took to their jobs with enthusiasm, showing up to work on time and finding things to do without being told—sweeping up hair from the floor, tidying the tea cupboard, even arranging the fashion magazines in neatly fanned piles. The smiles on their faces when they greeted the customers seemed genuine, and no matter how sour the clients looked upon their arrival, they rarely left without a smile of their own.

By the second month, the empty spaces in the salon's appointment book gradually began filling with names, and Adjoa noticed that in addition to a steady flow of repeat clients—including Gifty and Comfort—more and more new customers were coming on the basis of referrals. As the number of clients picked up, the days passed by quickly, from the first tinkle of Gifty's bell signaling a visitor early in the morning until the last client left in the evening, as late as 10 P.M.

Adjoa set aside Monday evenings to go over the accounts for the previous week. Despite the increase in customers, she approached this task with a sense of dread, for her expenses still consistently outweighed her earnings. After all, her staff had to be paid every week, and, now that they were in the hot dry season, it was important to keep the salon air-conditioned despite the high cost of electricity. In addition to her transportation to and from the salon, there were seemingly endless miscellaneous expenses—tea bags and biscuits, hair products and cleaning supplies, magazines for waiting customers, flowers for the vase at the front desk, even a radio so customers could listen to the Adom FM station. The pain in her arm often flared as she pored over the accounts, aching so badly that it affected her writing, the numbers in the ledger coming out crooked and shaky.

But during the rest of the week, the busyness of the salon—the constant chatter of women's voices over the radio's music, the flowery smell of shampoo battling with the pungent odor of perm solutions, the commotion of the staff as they bustled around—made Adjoa feel active and useful, keeping her mind off arm pains and secrets.

Four months after opening her salon, Adjoa returned from a midday errand to find Kobby's bicycle leaning against the outside wall. At the sound of Gifty's bell, Yaa looked up from her station, her hands hovering over a client's head half covered in pink curlers. "Your brother came to see you," she announced.

"Where did he go?" Adjoa asked.

"I told him you'd be here soon, and he said he would run an errand across the street and come back."

Adjoa glanced across the street at the chemist's shop but didn't see her brother. Yaa hesitated, her hands still. "He looked around the shop with great interest. I assumed he was the brother you named the salon after. Look," she added, titling her head in the direction of the window, "here he comes now."

Kobby crossed the street, a small white plastic bag in his hand. Adjoa greeted him as he stepped inside and offered him a cup of tea, which he turned down. "I can't stay long," he explained. "I just thought I'd pop by to say hello and have a look. The salon looks nice. Very clean."

"Thank you," Adjoa said.

He paused, throwing a glance in the direction of the other women. Though they all seemed intent on their tasks—Yaa had returned her attention to her client's curlers, Suzie was giving a manicure to a secretary who worked down the street, and Sylvia meticulously swept hair from the floor—none of them were chatting as they usually did. "I'm running late," Kobby said. "Will you walk outside with me?"

Once they were outside, Kobby turned to her. "As I said, Adjoa, the salon looks nice. But how is the business side going?"

Of course, this was why he'd come by. If anything, she should be surprised he hadn't come earlier. "It's fine, Kobby. I'm getting more and more clients every day."

"You look tired. Do you ever rest?"

Instead of answering, Adjoa shrugged her shoulders.

"I was thinking," he said, "that I could come by one evening to help you look over your ledger."

Adjoa felt her body stiffening. "It's only been four months, Kobby. I have another two."

"I just thought maybe you could use some help."

"No," she said, her voice sounding harsher than she meant it to. "I don't need any help."

Kobby stood next to his bicycle, looking down at her. In addition to being the eldest, he'd always been the biggest of her brothers, towering over her and Kojo. As a teenager, his build had made him look more clumsy than intimidating. Even now, holding the tiny bag in his oversized hand, he seemed ungainly, an awkward giant. She felt a moment of compassion: he, too, carried a heavy burden, having to oversee their large family, mediating every row. She hadn't meant to speak so brusquely to him.

Adjoa pointed at the bag and asked in a conciliatory tone what he'd purchased.

"Chloroquine, for Abigail," Kobby said, referring to his eldest daughter. "Whenever one of the children gets a headache now, Bernice treats them for malaria. I suppose once you've lost a family member to it. . . ." His voice trailed off.

Kobby's wife, Bernice, had an even larger family than theirs. Watching the traffic pass by, Adjoa idly tried to remember what family member Bernice had lost to malaria.

Then she looked up at Kobby, saw how he stared at her, and realized that of course he was referring to Kojo.

"He didn't die of malaria, did he, Adjoa?" he said, not taking his eyes off her.

"Yes, he did," she said, trying to hold his gaze. "Of course he did."

Kobby raised his hand as if he were about to touch her shoulder, then dropped it. His voice came out almost a whisper. "What are you hiding, Adjoa?"

Adjoa felt the old pain in her arm flare up and looked away. Inside the salon, the girls were busy with their tasks and their pink smocks looked bright and happy. Maybe, maybe it would be all right to tell her eldest brother the truth. Despite his clumsiness, their family trusted him to be steady and wise. It might even be a relief to lay down this burden. But, no, telling Kobby the truth—telling anyone— would be a betrayal of Kojo's memory. It would stir up too many things that were better left hidden. She hadn't had a choice then, and she didn't have one now.

"I'm as much your brother as Kojo was," he was telling her, "and he was as much my brother as yours. You can tell me the truth."

But Kobby was wrong. He would never understand the depth of the bond that had tied her—that still tied her—to her twin. A car pulled into a space in front of the salon, and Adjoa was relieved to recognize one of her clients, a wealthy woman who came weekly for touch-ups.

As Suzie came bounding out of the salon, flashing her gap-toothed smile to greet their client, Adjoa turned to Kobby. "I'm sorry, brother," she said, hoping her voice sounded properly apologetic. "You can see how busy we are. I really ought to return to work."

After she'd ushered her customer inside, Adjoa worked in a haze the rest of the afternoon. Though she automatically welcomed her clients, she barely kept an eye on Yaa and the apprentices. From time to time, she futilely shook her arm to stop the throbbing as she tended to someone's hair.

At the end of the day, she told Sylvia—whose turn it was to mop the floor—that she could leave early, deferring the mopping to the following morning. Once she was alone, Adjoa switched off the radio, sank down on one of the cushioned chairs, and put her head into her trembling hands.

She had come so close to telling Kobby the truth, so close to betraying her twin.

Adjoa stood up, rocking her aching arm against her chest as if it were a baby, and began pacing the room. If only she could go back in time to when she and Kojo lived in Abidjan, back far enough when she could still have made him return to Accra with her, even without the money they needed for the business. She, of all people, should have seen through her twin brother to know what he was up to. But she hadn't *wanted* to see it—it was as simple and terrible as that. And now she blamed herself for not having paid more attention to how shifty Kojo's acquaintances had become, not searching their single-room house to find the gun he'd bought, not figuring out that the hostile city they lived in had turned him into the kind of man who used the power of a gun to take things that didn't belong to him.

The first night he hadn't come home, she'd stayed up all night, waiting. The next day, she skipped work to search for him, trying to locate his friends, asking them if they knew anything, anything at all that would help her find him. Afraid he'd been mugged and beaten, or wounded in a late-night bus accident at Carrefour de la Mort, she checked the hospitals. When she couldn't find him there, she knew she would have to try the police station next, in case he'd lost his ID again. By then, she was so exhausted she fell into a deep sleep, waking up with a stiff right arm as if she'd slept on it all night.

Early the next morning, she took the *woro woro* to the police station and learned they'd been looking for her. The policeman ushered her by her elbow into the windowless room where a body lay on a wooden table, wearing torn and bloodied clothing. Kojo always wore his clothes neat and ironed, even if they were just jeans and a T-shirt, and she wanted to run from the room, yelling, "That's not Kojo, that's not my brother." But the policeman held her elbow firmly, and her eyes finally traveled up to the face—bruised and beaten, one side deep purple, swollen to double its usual size.

Even in that grotesque state, she recognized his face.

She reached out to touch the top of her brother's head, running her hand down the side of his face and neck, along his strong shoulder. Only then did she notice that his right arm lay at an impossible angle, forming a backward arc as if broken in several places. She began to scream, the sounds escaping from a hollow space inside her she'd never known existed, and the cursing policeman yanked her, kicking and thrashing, away from the room and her brother's crushed body.

The brain never forgets—it just hides things.

Adjoa stood in the middle of the salon and waited for the frenzied beating of her heart to slow down. At the time of Kojo's death she'd been so sure that she had no choice but to bury him in the city he'd grown to despise. His body was too broken to be fixed by even the most skilled mortician, so she couldn't take him home without the family learning about his fall from grace. Since she hadn't been able to save her brother, she would have to do what she could to save his name. Even if her choice was wrong—and she still wasn't sure it was—it couldn't be undone now. Telling the truth would only make things worse, would only reopen old wounds and inflict new ones on the family. And most of all, it wouldn't bring Kojo back. All she had now was the salon she'd named after him. And because it was the only thing she had left, she would do everything in her power to keep it. Look at how far it had already come, almost entirely by her own efforts.

As her eyes swept over the salon, they stopped at the sight

of her reflection in one of the salon mirrors. She took a single step toward the mirror, then several more, until she saw her face up close. With shock, she took in how much she'd aged—several strands of gray hair on either side of her part, dark half-moons under her eyes, and the skin on her neck no longer taut with youth.

How could she have passed these salon mirrors so many times a day without looking, without really *seeing* herself? It occurred to Adjoa that Kojo had always been her mirror, and because she still pictured him as a young man—his mouth erupting into a rakish grin—she'd been oblivious to the signs of her own aging. The face looking back at her now in the harsh fluorescent light was that of a stranger whose features held a determined, steadfast expression. It was the look she would have seen on the face of someone she encountered on the street who called her by name and then, realizing Adjoa didn't recognize her, was preparing to say, Don't you know who I am?

# Waiting for Solomon

The morning of their arrival in Bahir Dar, Ophelia sat next to her husband, Philip, in the back seat of a taxi, wondering what Solomon was doing at that same moment. As the car coughed its way up the gravel driveway, she pictured him sleeping in the crib he shared with another baby, their bodies instinctively curled against each other like puppies, oblivious to the crying of the other children or the orphanage's stale smell of sweat and dirty diapers.

The taxi driver made a sudden turn as he pulled to an abrupt halt in front of the hotel, flinging Ophelia against her husband. Philip's hands flew out to catch her, and Ophelia felt his fingers dig into her arms. From the front seat of the taxi, Janice turned around to ask, "You two lovebirds all right back there?"

They'd met Janice by chance in Addis Ababa—a fellow American, a single woman who'd lived in Africa for sixteen years and now worked in Senegal. She'd come to adopt a

baby from the same orphanage as Ophelia and Philip, running into a similar bureaucratic snafu with one of the min-
istries. They all hired a local lawyer who promised he'd fix
the problem in four or five days, a week at most. He encouraged them to explore Ethiopia while he took care of things,
speaking in such a cheerful tone that Ophelia wondered if
the glitch wasn't a total fabrication, a standard ploy used by
the government to boost the tourism industry.

It was Janice who talked them into going to Bahir Dar,
reminding them that adoptive parents should learn as much
as possible about their child's country of origin. She told
them it was just a short flight from Addis; they could get
there, visit the monasteries and the waterfall, and be back
within three days.

Ophelia had quickly pegged Janice as a know-it-all, one
of those Africaphiles who'd started out in the Peace Corps
and never left the continent. She'd learned to recognize them
by their bad hair and leathery skin, by the way they tried out
local phrases on waiters in restaurants. Even though none of
them had visited Ethiopia before, Janice had somehow found
out the best places to eat and which churches were worth
visiting, and she rattled off useless factoids about the Queen
of Sheba, the Italian occupation, and Haile Selassie.

But Ophelia hadn't come for tourism or side trips to
Bahir Dar. All she wanted was to continue their vigil in
Addis, visiting ten-month-old Solomon at the orphanage in
the morning and waiting at the hotel in the afternoon for the

lawyer's call that everything was settled, that they could take him back to Kenya, where they currently lived.

Philip, however, had insisted. "Come on, Ophelia, it's our last chance to just get away. Solomon's doing fine at the orphanage, and nothing's going to change in the next three days. Besides," he added, "it'll be a good distraction. For both of us."

She'd given in, finally, not because of Philip's words but because Addis depressed her even more than the orphanage: the hordes of people on the streets, dressed in sweaters with holes in their elbows, and the beggars that scuttled up to their taxi windows at every stoplight, some without hands and others without legs, propelling themselves on low wheeled carts. There were beggars in Nairobi, of course, but they were nowhere near as plentiful or aggressive. Worst of all were the children, in tattered clothes and matted hair, who stalked the streets near the Hilton with their arms outstretched. Even though Janice had explained that many of the children posed as orphans, that their parents actually encouraged them to beg, Ophelia felt her heart lurch every time they approached her to chant in accented English, "Mother father dead, stomach zero."

After lunch at the hotel, Janice led Ophelia and Philip down the steps to a dock on Lake Tana, where she'd negotiated a motorboat to take them to the islands to visit monasteries and churches dating back, she explained, as far as the six-teenth century.

"You doing okay?" Philip whispered, when Janice's back was turned.

Ophelia nodded. Though his words seemed kind, his tone hinted at a recurring accusation that she was impossible to please—a claim she felt was unjustified. She'd done her best to adjust to living in Africa, first in Malawi, and now in Kenya. But try as she might, she could never get used to the signs of human suffering, not to mention the stench of sewage when a breeze blew into their car window as they drove past the shanty towns. She hated the fact that her white skin automatically labeled her as privileged, mak-ing her a constant target for people asking for money—not just beggars but the servants, too, who regularly asked for advances on their salary. How could she say no? At home, she felt robbed of her privacy by the ever-present cook and houseboy, the sounds of their conversations in Kiswahili viscerally grating against her nerves. Of course the hardest thing—the one thing that was finally about to change—had been their childlessness. Just thinking about Solomon, the warmth of his skin, the funny bed-head shapes of his wispy hair, made Ophelia soften, letting go of Philip's innu-endo. Maybe he *was* just trying to be nice.

They climbed onto the small motorboat with benches on either side, a plastic sheet that rested on four poles shielding them from the sun. Philip sat next to Ophelia on one side of the boat, while Janice took a seat on the other side, next to the Ethiopian man she'd introduced as their guide. The driver of the boat pointed to the orange life jackets tucked under their benches and motioned for them to put them on before he turned on the engine.

"What a nice day for a boat ride," Janice said, over the sound of the motor, brushing her rust-brown hair away from her eyes as the wind blew it across her face.

With a flush of satisfaction, Ophelia noticed a hint of gray roots. "A *beautiful* day," she agreed, looking over at her husband to make sure he was listening. "Look over there," she said, pointing at a flock of pelicans with pouched beaks and a faint pink hue to the feathers on their backs, skirting the surface of the water before they flew into the clear sky.

"Gorgeous," Philip agreed, placing his arm around Ophelia's shoulder.

"Bahir Dar is well known for birds," Janice said, as they continued to chug toward the nearest island. "We'll be seeing a lot more on this trip."

After they landed at the first island, they followed the guide uphill through a wooded area to a clearing with a modest round church, the eaves of its conical tin roof lined with tiny metal decorations that looked like bells. They were greeted by a short monk, barely five feet high, wearing a cap, a long robe down to his plastic-sandal-clad feet, and what looked like a blanket draped over his shoulders. He ushered them inside and pointed at vividly colored paintings on the walls depicting biblical scenes, which he explained in heavily accented English that Ophelia couldn't understand.

Alongside benign pictures of men with Ethiopian features riding horses and sitting on thrones, there were gruesome images depicting beheadings and hangings.

Ophelia lingered in front of a painting of the Virgin Mary holding a cross in one hand and baby Jesus in the other. The baby's round dark eyes reminded her of Solomon, the way his eyes had widened as he'd clutched her when it was time to leave at the end of their last visit. She pictured herself holding him again, this time at their house in Nairobi, in the nursery she'd painted periwinkle blue, whispering his name over and over. Solomon, though: it sounded so—well, solemn. Before she'd found out she couldn't have children, they'd agreed that if they had a son they would name him Philip, but Philip had declared a few days ago that it sounded too Western, too British upper-crust, and the baby should keep his given name of Solomon. They could shorten it to Solly, she decided, repeating the name in her mind. Solly. Or did that sound too much like sorry? She would discuss it with Philip later.

After they took their leave of the monk and started back to the boat, Janice asked Philip about his work in Kenya. Ophelia half listened to him describe his desk job at the embassy, launching into a tangent about the role of politics in foreign aid—a diatribe she'd heard before but that Janice prodded into a prolonged conversation. Once they were in the boat again, their discussion turned to a project Janice was starting in Senegal that had something to do with AIDS, and Ophelia tuned out entirely.

Until Malawi, everything in her life had been on track. She'd been raised to marry a suitable husband, attending a private all-girls high school in Connecticut, followed by Vassar College, where she met Philip. After graduation, she followed him to Washington, D.C., where he studied at Georgetown's School of Foreign Service while she worked as a paralegal, refusing to move in with him until they married. After the wedding and before his first posting to Malawi, they stayed on in D.C. for four years—easy, blissful years that now felt to her like they'd been part of someone else's life.

At first, she welcomed the role of foreign-service spouse. Things had started to fall apart only when she learned, after their first year in Lilongwe, that she was infertile. At the time, Philip retreated into a shell like a crab, throwing himself into his job and ignoring her free-fall toward an emotional breakdown. Far from her family in the United States and grappling with her grief alone, she finally threatened him, as a last resort, with divorce—a huge gamble, of course, but it had paid off. Philip snapped into action, crawling out of his cave and working with her to draw up and discuss a list of their options to form a family. Though none of the items on their list had appealed to her—each one reeked of desperation—she realized now that the simple act of making the list had at least given her back a sense of control. After the ultimatum, the topic of divorce never resurfaced, although Ophelia sometimes noticed a new tone of guardedness that crept into their conversations. When the notion of severing their marriage occasionally still bobbed up in her mind unbidden, she quickly pushed the thought away, reminding herself that everything would change once they had a child.

They had tried fertility treatments—the first item on their list—for nearly three years before Ophelia decided they were as useless as they were painful and finally gave up. They'd discussed in vitro fertilization and even a surrogate, but both ideas appalled her and she'd made him cross them off the list, leaving the final alternative: adoption. At first she assumed they would adopt an American baby, until they realized how difficult that would be while they lived overseas. Philip pointed out that there were more African babies in need of a home anyway, and once they'd made that decision, they quickly learned that Ethiopia was the most organized African country when it came to international adoptions.

With a jolt their boat docked at a second island, and they followed the guide down a path, this time leading to a large arch made of rocks and a tin awning. Smiling at Philip as if at a shared joke, the guide lifted a plastic tarp draped over a hand-lettered sign that read: NO ENTRANCE FOR LADY.

"Well, I'm no lady," said Janice, laughing, "so does that mean I can go in?"

Philip chuckled. "I think they mean women in general, Janice, lady or not."

"So they're afraid of the effects of the weaker sex on the monks?" asked Janice. "Well, I think you should go ahead and look it over, just to report back to us what goes on in a men-only monastery."

"I couldn't do that," said Philip. "It would make me a traitor to my gender." He was smiling, his white teeth flashing through his beard. As Janice threw her head back and laughed, Ophelia suddenly wondered if this woman was flirting with her husband. She eyed Janice surreptitiously, taking in the sun-damaged skin and obviously dyed hair—she was clearly well into her forties. Janice couldn't seriously entertain the notion that Philip might be interested in her. Not only was she nearly a decade older than he was, but there was the basic fact of Philip's personality—he just wasn't the unfaithful type. Still, Ophelia began to wonder why Philip, who was usually an introvert, seemed to enjoy conversing with this stranger

Janice had stopped laughing and was pointing at something in the tree over Ophelia's head. Her voice came out in a whisper. "Look there. See those two birds?"

"I do," Philip said, his voice as low as Janice's. "Look at the bright red mark over their beaks."

Ophelia peered into the dense leaves but didn't see anything. "What birds?" she asked, her voice coming out louder than she'd intended. As if to answer her question, a loud rustling noise erupted from overhead, and a flurry of white and black feathers flashed by before the birds disappeared in search of a more private refuge.

———

That evening, Ophelia and Philip found Janice in the dining hall, reading a book.

"I think I figured out what those birds were that we saw today," she told them, as they sat down next to her.

"Oh, yeah?" said Philip, reaching for a menu in the middle of their table.

"I already ordered," Janice said.

Ophelia was gratified by the hint of a frown on Philip's face as his hand still hovered over the menus.

"I'm sorry," Janice said, "should I not have done that? You guys were late, and it gets shared anyway, so I just ordered *zilzil tibbs*, *doro watt*, and some lentils. A bit of everything."

Philip seemed to think this over. "Beef, chicken, and beans—you're right, a bit of everything," he said, nodding. "You're very efficient, Janice."

Ophelia was too surprised that he'd recognized the Amharic names of the dishes to figure out if his compliment had been tongue-in-cheek or sincere.

A waiter approached Philip and handed him a different menu. "Madam said the mister would order wine?"

Philip took the menu with exaggerated casualness, perusing it slowly and finally asking if they would like to try an Ethiopian wine. Ophelia shrugged her shoulders, but Janice was more enthusiastic. "Great idea," she said. "I hear they're not the best, but it'll be fun to try."

Philip ordered the Axumite wine and handed the menu back to the waiter, who retreated noiselessly. Janice held up the book she'd been reading and pointed to a detailed drawing of an unattractive, stocky bird speckled black and white with a red thatch on its forehead.

"Yep, that looks like the ones we saw," Philip said, as Janice flipped the book over so she could read from it.

"Here's what it says: 'Banded Barbets sing in pairs in such a synchronized fashion that it is impossible to tell which note is coming from which bird. Moreover, they tend to stay in mated pairs, nesting in tree cavities they've excavated with their solid beaks.'"

"Mate for life, you mean?" Ophelia interrupted, throwing a half smile in Philip's direction. She was rewarded by a smile back, an unexpected gift—she'd forgotten how perfectly straight his teeth were. Before Janice could answer, they were interrupted by the waiter, who returned to their table with the bottle of wine and ceremoniously opened it. He poured a few swallows of the dark red liquid into Philip's glass.

Philip took a sip and made a slight grimace. "It's awfully sweet," he said, "but what the hey—it's a taste of Ethiopia."

He nodded at the waiter, who filled their glasses. Ophelia reached for hers and held it up. "Cheers," she said, hardly waiting for the others to raise their glasses before she took a deep swallow, feeling her jaw tighten at the syrupy flavor. Janice took a sip and returned to perusing her book—though she no longer read out loud—while Philip seemed engrossed with the label on their wine bottle. Ophelia took another gulp from her glass, trying unsuccessfully to get the wine down her throat without tasting it, almost gagging at the cloying sweetness. Still, once it traveled into her stomach she felt a delicious warmth coursing through her body. Another swallow and she imagined knots and skeins of muscle loosening in her shoulders and arms and legs. She looked at Janice again, hunched over her book, and saw a middle-aged single woman married to her career and engrossed with dull trivia like birds. Why had she let Janice make her so tense? After all, she'd come to the same decision as Ophelia to adopt—at least they had that much in common. The only difference was that Janice had made her decision knowing she would raise her child without the help of a husband.

Janice snapped the book shut. "Well," she said, "I guess that wasn't so interesting after all."

"It would be to an ornithologist," Philip said, refilling everyone's glass. "Or another bird." From his joking tone, Ophelia could tell that he was being indulgent. Had he been feigning interest in Janice's conversations all day?

Their waiter came bearing an enormous tray that he placed in the center of the table. They watched him spoon strips of beef, shiny with oil, onto *injera* bread spread across the tray, followed by yellow lentils and a red sauce with chicken and a boiled egg that he split open. Ophelia suddenly felt ravenous, reaching in with the others to tear off pieces of *injera* and using it to scoop up strips of beef or a chunk of chicken that slipped easily from the bone. They chewed in silence until Philip turned the topic of conversation to the monastery that they hadn't seen, conjecturing what an all-male monastery might be like. "Sports on cable TV every night? Each monk gets his own remote control?"

Laughing along with Janice at his jokes, Ophelia couldn't remember the last time Philip had seemed so relaxed. It was probably the ridiculously horrible but potent wine, she thought, giggling to herself as he ordered a second bottle. She didn't even mind when Janice and Philip veered the conversation back into African politics, debating U.S. support to the hard-line Ethiopian leadership.

"It's like the cold war has been replaced by the war on terror," Philip said, his knee brushing against Ophelia's under the table for a second. At his touch, a sudden current coursed through her body, a giddy attraction she hadn't felt in months, possibly years.

"You okay?" he asked. "You look flushed."

She wanted to say she was much more than okay, but she knew it would sound silly, so she merely smiled and placed her right hand on his arm, letting it rest there for several minutes as Janice and Philip continued their conversation.

Once they'd drained their glasses and emptied the tray of all its food except for a few torn shreds of sauce-soaked *injera*, Janice reminded them with a yawn that they were leaving early the next morning to visit the falls. "We may as well get some sleep while we can," she added, with a smile at Ophelia. "Lord knows we won't be getting enough once we get our babies home."

"We've decided Solomon's going to be the perfect baby and sleep whenever we want him to," Ophelia declared, with a laugh that sounded oddly distant. As she pushed back her chair and stood up, she felt a rush of vertigo and nearly stumbled. How many glasses of wine had she drunk? She hadn't been paying attention. It didn't matter, anyway; Philip would get her back to their room. She reached for his arm to steady herself and heard him murmur into her ear, "Steady now."

His whispered breath felt hot against her ear and she nestled against him, letting her body lean on him more heavily than she needed to as they said good-bye to Janice and walked back to their room. Something had shifted during this seemingly ordinary evening. The tiniest of gestures— her shared smile with Philip, his jokes, their touching knees, even her moment of empathy for Janice—had all somehow added up to something bigger, something monumental and life-changing. But what exactly did it mean? Had she caught a glimpse of how good their life would be with Solomon? Or was she merely finally ready to move on, to put the last few stressful years behind her? She knew she hadn't always been easy to be with during this period—at times a bit critical, even irritable—but they had done it, they had come through intact, and as soon as they had Solomon they could start their new life together.

Watching Philip fumble with the key to their room, Ophelia wanted to reassure him that she would change back into the person she once was—no, into someone better. Once the baby joined them, she would be the best mother and wife he could wish for, they would be a family, and everything would be fine. As he pushed open the door and steered her inside by her elbow, she smiled at his strong and steady touch, realizing that she didn't need to say anything. He already knew.

A few minutes later, as she brushed her teeth in the bathroom, cleaning off the film of sugar from the night's wine, Philip called out, "That was a nice day, wasn't it?"

"Mmm-hmm," she agreed.

"I'm glad we came," he said. "It's good to see a bit more of Ethiopia than just the capital, don't you think?"

Ophelia came out of the bathroom and walked toward him, brushing up against him so closely that he backed up a step, flush against the wall. "Let's not talk about that right now," she murmured.

Philip looked surprised. "I just meant . . ."

She leaned forward to kiss him, pressing him into the wall. She felt his arms fold around her, pulling her against his chest. Their kisses were sloppy, her lips wet from his saliva and hers, her cheek scratched by his beard—the kind of messy, frenzied kissing that normally left her cold, but this time only spurred her on. Suddenly desperate to feel his bare skin against hers, she yanked at his shirt, fumbling with the buttons as he pulled her toward the bed.

Moments later, holding him inside and riding on top of him with her thighs pressed tightly against his waist, she closed her eyes and began rocking, slowly at first and then with increasing fierceness until she felt herself sinking, releasing, and finally rushing toward a wave of pleasure she hadn't allowed herself to feel in years. Somewhere, beyond the sound of Philip's panting, she heard a guttural moan that sounded like it came from far away rather than from her own throat.

Afterward, she threw herself down onto the sheet next to him, exhausted and sweating, reclaiming her breath until the rhythm of their heavy breathing joined into a single song.

Ophelia woke up to the cawing of a bird outside their window, the insides of her head pushing against her skull, her tongue feeling as if it were coated by a thick fungus. When she opened her eyes, the light stabbed at them, making them water. She heard Philip humming in the bathroom. Her eyes scanned the room as she struggled to remember where they were, until it all came back—the plane ride, the outing on the lake, last night with Philip, and the reality that she was physically even farther away from Solomon than she'd been the day before. No, she corrected herself, Solly.

"Ah, good, you're up," said Philip, emerging from the bathroom fully dressed. "I was getting ready to wake you. We're meeting Janice for breakfast in ten minutes, and the van is supposed to come by the hotel at nine."

She sat up in the bed, a wave of nausea breaking over her.

He paused to sit down on the edge of the bed. "Ophelia," he said. "Last night? That was . . . a nice surprise."

He leaned down to kiss her on the mouth, but fearing her breath was rancid she offered him her cheek instead. She pulled her knees against her chest and laid her head down on them.

"Hung over?" he asked. She felt one of his hands touching her feet.

She groaned.

"Want some water?"

"Yes," she said. "Please."

He handed her a bottle of lukewarm mineral water from the nightstand, and she gulped down several swigs. As she passed it back to Philip, she finally looked over at him.

"Thank you."

"Are you going to be all right?" he asked, placing the bottle back on the nightstand.

She nodded. "I think so. I just need a long hot shower. But I don't think I'm up for breakfast. Maybe you can bring me a slice of toast, and I'll try to eat that before we head out to the falls."

"Sure, no problem," he said, as he looked at his watch. "Oops, better head out. Don't want to keep Janice waiting."

"No, you wouldn't want to do that," she said, sounding more sarcastic than she'd meant to, though he didn't seem to notice, kissing her again—this time on the forehead—and bounding out with a level of energy she hadn't seen in him in months, maybe longer. Was it the sex? she asked herself. Am I that good? Or was it something else? She remembered how hopeful she'd felt the night before, walking back to their room, how sure she'd been that everything would work out once they became a real family. Had he felt that, too?

She looked around the hotel room, at the wooden

furniture, the tiny desk against the opposite wall, and then at the window. Philip had opened the curtains halfway, and from the bed she caught a glimpse of the view. A thick layer of fog hovered outside, obscuring the lake. She felt another surge of nausea, last night's meal and the lethally sweet wine churning in her stomach. *Just get through this day,* she told herself. *Tomorrow we'll be on our way back to Addis, and then we can finally pick up Solly.* If all she had to do to hold him in her arms again, to bring him home, was get through today, she could do that. Easily. She threw off the covers and headed to the bathroom.

By the time she sat next to Philip in the van that would take them to the falls, Ophelia felt only marginally better, despite the pleasant, cool air outside. On top of her hangover, she'd discovered when she went to the bathroom that her period had started, and though the pain reliever she took to ward off cramps had helped her headache, it seemed to exacerbate the nausea, her stomach somersaulting as the van took off with a lurch. Two rows ahead of them, sitting among a handful of locals who were hitching a ride, Janice elicited raucous laughter when she asked them if they, too, were going to the waterfalls, unself-consciously pantomiming water falling over rocks. From the front seat, the driver called out to them, "You need guide for Tis Abay? We find you guide."

Janice turned around in her seat and looked back at

them. "We don't really need guides," she said. "According to the guidebook, the path is pretty clear. But it gives the Ethiopians some business. What do you think?"

"Absolutely," Philip agreed. "Let's hire a guide for Tis Abay."

"I thought you'd say that, but I wanted to check." She turned back and yelled to the driver, "That would be great!"

Ophelia looked at Philip. "What was that you said?"

"What, Tis Abay?"

She nodded.

"It's the local name for the falls," he said. "Janice explained it to me this morning. It means Smoke of the Nile. To describe the mist from the falls, you know? It looks like smoke. . . ."

The van swerved, making her stomach lurch again.

"Yeah, I get it," she said, turning to look outside the window at the landscape, a trick her mother taught her as a child for whenever she had motion sickness. In the distance, clouds floated low in the wan blue sky, throwing long shadows across the hills. They passed an empty plot of rocky dirt, followed by a grassy area and a large tree, then a donkey carrying a load of wood, being led by an old man who held a walking stick, a dirty cloth draped around his torso like the priest at the monastery. What a desolate scene, biblical even, as if nothing had changed for the last twenty centuries. What a different life Solly would lead with them than if he stayed in Ethiopia, if his mother hadn't given him up.

By the time the van pulled over for good, they had already

dropped off several of the Ethiopians along the way. The remaining ones tumbled out and dispersed in different directions, leaving the three Americans inside. Outside, several lanky young men wearing faded T-shirts rushed toward the driver, babbling loudly in Amharic. Janice stepped out and strolled around to the driver's side of the car to join the conversation, at which point the men fell into short English phrases—"I know best way" and "Tis Abay not far"—as Janice negotiated which of them would guide them.

Ophelia stayed seated, waiting for her stomach to settle as she watched Philip unfurl his legs and stand up as best he could in the van, his back curved under the low ceiling. When he shuffled toward the door, Ophelia felt a moment of panic. Without thinking, she reached up and grabbed his arm. He spun around, a surprised expression on his face. "Are you all right? What's the matter?"

What could she say, Don't leave the van? Let's forget the falls, turn around, go straight to the airport, pick up the baby in Addis, and go home? She knew how silly she would sound, how melodramatic, so instead she took a deep breath and forced a smile. "I'm fine," she said, letting go of his arm. "It's nothing."

Philip furrowed his brow for a second, then turned and stepped out of the van. As he shook out his legs, a small girl approached him with her hand palm up. She wore a long skirt discolored with dirt, a leather amulet around her neck, and her hair in disheveled braids. At the sight of the girl's face, the bright eyes and beautiful Ethiopian features, Ophelia lost her breath. Why not take her home, too, she thought impulsively, an older sister for Solly? She could already picture them playing together in the backyard of their house.

But Philip brushed past the girl—had he even noticed her?—to join Janice, leaving Ophelia alone in the van. The girl noticed Ophelia's stare and leaned forward eagerly, pushing her hand toward the open window. Half expecting to hear the same chant she'd heard in Addis—"Mother father dead, stomach zero"—she was stunned when the girl clearly said, "*Innateye.*"

It was the only Amharic word that Ophelia knew, a word she'd been taught by a worker at the orphanage while she held Solomon.

The child repeated it again. "*Innateye.*" Mother.

From the front seat, the driver barked something in Amharic at the girl, and before Ophelia could stop her, she scampered away.

"Why did you do that?" she shouted at the driver, who shrugged and turned back to the negotiations with the guides. Ophelia turned to watch the girl cross the dirt road and grab the skirt hem of a woman—the girl's real mother, she knew instinctively—waiting for her on the other side. The woman carried a bucket on her head, her clothes as worn and faded as the child's. How stupid to assume the child needed a mother, needed *her.* And yet, how could that mother allow, even encourage, the girl's begging? She would never— Ophelia clutched at her stomach.

She was not a mother. At least, not yet.

Janice had chosen two guides for them—both of them young men with slender frames under their loose T-shirts, different only in their height. The taller one led the way down a muddy path between rocks and patches of dark green grass, and an occasional footbridge made of sticks. They marched in a single file, Janice following the guide, then Philip, then Ophelia, and, finally, the second guide.

To keep up with the others, Ophelia had to walk faster than she wanted to, her white sneakers getting muddy, her irritation at the wetness seeping into her toes heightened by the prattle of Philip's and Janice's voices ahead of her. The path came to an abrupt halt at a river, where the guides helped them climb into a rickety metal boat painted light blue. Thankfully, Philip and Janice put their conversation on hiatus, while Ophelia, who still felt queasy, tried to keep her eyes focused on a tree as the boat chugged across the brown water.

On the other side of the river, as if by magic, a group of children emerged from the bushes. The girls wore long skirts that swished as they leaped barefoot from rock to rock with uncanny agility. The boys carried walking sticks and wore shorts and matching jackets, dirty and torn, made from thick dark-blue fabric. They were young—the eldest could not have been older than eight—and Ophelia tried to imagine what kind of parent would let a child roam around in the wild without supervision. She counted at least twenty of them, each looking as neglected and unwanted as the next. How outrageous—scandalous, even—that despite the many discarded children in this country, she and Philip had to jump over so many hurdles just to take home a single one.

The children followed them in a loose feral pack until one of the guides stopped and pointed to an enormous cliff in the distance across a deep lush-green valley. Three thin streams of water trickled down the overhang, hardly what could be called a waterfall.

"This is it?" Ophelia said. "Is he sure?"

"I don't know what to say," Janice said. "My friends who came here last year said it was gorgeous."

Ophelia looked at her and then back at the sickly falls. "This is why we trudged through all this mud?"

"I'm sorry," Janice said, her eyes wide. "They mentioned that sometimes the water gets circumvented for hydroelectric power, but I didn't think to ask about it at the hotel."

Before Ophelia could say anything else, Philip chimed in. "Don't worry about it, Janice. It's not your fault. Besides, it's still a nice view."

He asked Ophelia and Janice to pose with the two guides and snapped a picture, several of the children sneaking into the shot at the last minute. One of the girls reached out to touch Ophelia's arm, running away again with a laugh. How impish, she thought, even though it was not a word she normally used. She imagined the children living on their own in the outdoors, sprites in a fairy tale, their only protection the amulets they wore around their necks. Turning to look across the valley at the cliff, she felt a heightening of her senses, as if the cool, sharp air were turning her previously addled and hungover brain into a finely tuned receptor. The smell of the damp earth accosted her nose, the patter of the children's Amharic formed a seemingly intelligible rhythm to her ears, and her eyes focused with such clarity on the green grass at the foot of the cliff that she could make out every one of the grazing brown- and black-spotted cows below, even though they looked tiny as ants from where she stood.

After several minutes in which none of the adults spoke, Janice finally said, "I guess there's not much point in sticking around."

"Okay," Philip said, "let's head back."

This time, Ophelia walked behind the first guide, followed by Philip and Janice, their conversation replaced by the chatter of the children around them. She strode with renewed energy, as if Solomon himself were waiting at the end of the path. Tomorrow, they would return to Addis, the final step to becoming a real family. As she picked her way down the muddy trail, she pictured him once again, his stubby arms reaching out to her, until the image was pushed away by the loud shouts of the children.

She turned to see two boys arguing, the larger one pushing the smaller one, who responded by attacking with his walking stick. When the older boy deflected the stick with his own, they began sparring with the makeshift weapons, frenziedly jabbing at each other, their sticks making terrifying cracking noises. Tracks of tears had begun to form down the younger boy's cheeks, and the surrounding children yelled with increasing vigor—either out of fear or to egg on the boys, she couldn't tell which.

The taller guard flung his arm out protectively in front of Ophelia, his eyes focused on the brawl. She glanced over at Philip, to make sure that he was all right, only to notice that he had flung out his arm in the same gesture as the guard, except his arm was protecting Janice.

Ophelia and Philip's eyes locked for several seconds. She realized she was holding her breath. He kept his eyes on her as he lowered his arm, and she felt herself finally exhale.

Years later, living alone in the United States with Solly, she would remember the look in Philip's eyes before she turned away—a mixture of surprise and comprehension. She would remember the singing of birds in the distance and realize that the children must have already turned quiet. Between the moment when Philip lowered his arm and the earth-shattering one that followed it, all of her half-formed thoughts about Africa became as clear and sharp as the air around her, and she understood at last why she hated living there. It wasn't, as she had once thought, the poverty and constant harassment for money. It wasn't the heat or the dirt or the cacophony of foreign tongues. What she finally understood was that nothing felt safe to her—not her marriage, not her physical self, not even her sanity—and without that feeling of safety, she could never create a home for herself and her child.

Thinking back on this moment, she would know that it

couldn't have lasted as long as it seemed. She would understand it could only have been a second or two, the time it
took for her to look away from her husband and back to the
fight between the two boys. The older boy stood over the
younger one, his stick raised. By then, even the birds had
stopped singing, the silence so complete that she could hear
the whistle of the rod as it came down with a crack against
the younger boy's skull.

# Life Is Like a Mirror

An hour after her friend Gifty was declared Samuel's wife, Adjoa surveyed the crowd of guests dancing to highlife music and thought of the Akan expression "In this world we live in pairs." Everyone but me, she thought, as she watched Gifty, in her cloud of a white dress, dancing with her new husband, who wore a black tuxedo with a bowtie made of kente cloth.

Gifty's hair was holding up beautifully; even the tiny white silk flowers that Adjoa had woven into an amalgamation of twists and braids stayed firmly in place. As friend of the bride and owner of the Precious Brother Salon, Adjoa had gone to Gifty's house at five o'clock that morning to create her hairstyle, even though the previous night she'd been at the salon until almost midnight, overseeing her staff primp the female wedding guests.

Stifling a yawn, Adjoa continued to survey the dance floor. On the edge of the crowd, her friend and client, Comfort, danced with her two-year-old grandson, holding his small hands in hers as they swayed to the sound of Papa Shee singing "You're My Number One." Comfort's son, Ekow, was trying unsuccessfully to coax his American wife onto the dance floor, finally giving up and motioning for his young daughter instead. Seated alone, the white woman looked painfully self-conscious and out of place, and Adjoa couldn't help feeling an odd kinship with her; despite the beaming faces of the wedding guests and the loud, cheery music being played by the DJ, clearly neither of them felt like dancing.

Not that Adjoa wasn't happy for Gifty, nor was she ungrateful—even for a second—for her own thriving business. Her bleak mood had more to do with the fact that she had no one with whom to share her success. Being surrounded by couples and children at a wedding only served as a stinging reminder of her loneliness. Was she the only single, childless woman in Gifty's circle? Comfort was on her own, but a widow with grown children, so that didn't count. Earlier, Adjoa had met two of Gifty's nieces who were single, but they were young women with plenty of time to meet their mates. Adjoa, on the other hand, with her thirty-eight years, was quickly running out of time to form a family.

During her twenties and early thirties in Abidjan, there had been several suitors, but none of them had proven serious enough for Adjoa to embark on marriage. Besides, she'd been too busy working and planning with her twin brother, Kojo, to set up their beauty salon back in Accra. After she lost Kojo and returned home without him, all the toil of building a business had fallen on her; she'd been much too occupied to meet any marital prospects. Now that the business was finally on a solid footing, now that she could leave the salon in the hands of her competent staff whenever she wanted, it seemed all of the good men were taken—or married and looking for a mistress.

For months, Gifty had been encouraging her to go out and meet people, to find a good man like Samuel. But where were they, these good men? And, really, what was the point when the world was so unsafe, when the people you cared for could be snatched away in a single moment by fate? Why become attached to someone, only to eventually suffer the pain of losing him—and then, like Comfort, being alone again? If only Kojo had lived to see the salon! At the thought of her brother, Adjoa felt a dull ache in her right arm—the same phantom pain she'd been feeling off and on ever since his death, though it came with much less frequency now. She breathed in deeply and let out a slow sigh, the pain releasing as she exhaled. It was wrong to have such dreary thoughts at a friend's wedding, to infect a day of such joy with sadness and gloom. Better to slip out unnoticed amid the noise and gaiety.

Adjoa flipped open her mobile phone, pressed the number for Tony's Hiring Cars, and gave her location to the dispatcher. As she stood up and reached for her purse, she was aware of someone lowering himself into the empty seat next to hers. When she turned around, a man sat looking up at her, his legs blocking her exit.

"Oh," he said. "I hope you're not leaving because of me."

It was one of those ill-timed moments that could easily be misconstrued. She ought to sit down again, just out of politeness. But that would only make it look like he'd been right—that she'd started to leave because of him and was staying to prove him wrong.

The man smiled in an easy, relaxed manner, as if they already knew each other. He had an evenly shaped, round head, made all the more evident by his closely trimmed hair, which Adjoa could see from the stubble was partly gray; she guessed he was in his mid-forties. His skin tone was dark and smooth, the color of damp coffee grounds, and he was dressed in a blue suit that seemed slightly tight in the shoulders.

The man's smile had begun to falter by the time Adjoa finally answered him. "Not at all," she said. "I didn't . . . I mean, I was just getting ready to leave when you sat down."

"You're not having a good time?"

"No, it's been lovely. It's just I'm rather tired. . . ." She wasn't sure how to go on.

He seemed to take her hesitation as an invitation to chat. "You must be friends with the bride? Or family? If Samuel knew you, I'd have met you by now."

"Yes, I am—a friend of Gifty's, I mean," she said. "But I was just . . . if you'd be so kind as to move your. . . ." Even though she could feel his eyes on her, she kept her eyes locked on his legs, as if she could will them to move. Why was this man making her so nervous?

"Very well, then," he said, but instead of turning his legs sideways, he stood up and motioned in an easy, gentlemanly manner that she should pass.

Surprised by how tall he was, she walked past him wordlessly. "Why not have a quick dance before you leave?" he asked.

It had been so long since a man—and a handsome one at that—had shown any interest in Adjoa that she was caught off guard. "Someone's waiting for me—" She broke off with the flustered feeling that she was lying, even though someone *was* waiting for her—the driver of the car she'd just hired.

"Ah," the man said. "Now I understand."

"It's not . . . I didn't mean . . . ," she said, then thought better of it. Better to escape now, before she made an even bigger fool of herself, incapable as she seemed to be of completing a full sentence in front of this man.


Adjoa walked out of the air-conditioned hall and into the afternoon sun, berating herself as she paused to let her eyes adjust to the brightness. Why had she been so flustered? What was *wrong* with her?

Across the street, the pale-blue boxlike Tico looked out of place parked next to a row of black and gray Mercedes-Benzes and BMWs. The car door was marked TONY'S HIRING CARS in large dark-blue letters, with a phone number underneath. Adjoa waited for a van to pass before she crossed the road.

A year ago, she'd hired one of Tony's cars in response to a leaflet distributed at her salon, proclaiming Tony's Hiring Cars Guarantee the Lowest Rates in Town! The Safest and Most Courteous Drivers! Monthly Billing Available for Businesses! Adjoa didn't drive; she couldn't afford a car before and was too old to learn to drive now. But she'd grown tired of taking buses, and taxis were expensive. Tony had seemed like the answer to her prayers until his driver appeared in the tiny odd-looking car. But the driver had jumped out to open her door, and even if the Tico was cramped for someone with a generous build like Adjoa's, it was spotlessly clean inside. Afterward, she called other car services to see if she could find a comparable arrangement, but—true to Tony's leaflet—the others were more expensive and the drivers never as courteous or as prompt. She always came back to his service, finally entering into an agreement whereby she rang them whenever she needed a ride and his office sent a reasonable invoice at the end of each month— although for some reason she hadn't received one for the previous month.

Adjoa was surprised to see Tony climbing out of the driver's seat; normally one of his drivers came to pick her up. But it was unmistakably him, with his short, stocky build, topped by a shiny dome of a head.

"Good afternoon," he said, as he opened the passenger door, his eyebrows raised slightly in a look that reminded Adjoa of something or someone she couldn't place. It gave his greeting a quizzical quality, as if he were asking her whether her afternoon was indeed a good one.

"And a good afternoon to you, too," Adjoa answered; there was no trace of a question in *her* greeting. "You're driving today?"

"Absolutely," he said. "Asare is sick, and I can't let his car stay idle."

As Adjoa climbed into the backseat of the car, she felt the same twinge of embarrassment that hit her every time she climbed into one of Tony's Ticos. At first this reaction had surprised her; she didn't think of herself as vain. And yet there it was, every time, as niggling as the itch of a fresh mosquito bite. The one time she'd asked Tony if he ever thought of acquiring other kinds of cars for his fleet, he'd laughed good-naturedly. It didn't bother him, he said, that people made fun of his cars. For the price of one Toyota he could practically buy two Ticos, and two cars on the road—even if they were Ticos—made twice as much money as one.

After Tony climbed into his seat and started the car, Adjoa mentioned that she hadn't received the previous month's invoice. He promised to look into it, adding—as if one subject naturally led to the other—that she looked fashionable this afternoon. He kept his eyes on the road as Adjoa explained—in a raised voice so she could be heard over the motor—that she'd been at a friend's wedding.

Tony nodded, apparently satisfied by this information, and Adjoa contented herself with watching the passing scenery, a row of shops that sold textiles, car parts, and bathroom fixtures. They passed a young couple strolling underneath a flame tree bejeweled with orange-red blossoms, and Adjoa thought again of the tall man at Gifty's wedding. Why had she run away like a frightened mouse? Just twenty minutes ago she'd been lamenting her state of loneliness, and when the gentleman had asked her to dance she was so flustered that she'd left without even asking his name. How would she ever meet someone special if she didn't try?

Two weeks after Gifty's wedding, Adjoa was in the midst of another busy day at the Precious Brother Salon. The business had expanded considerably since she'd launched it two years ago. She now employed three hairdressers full-time—Yaa, who had been with her from the beginning, and Sylvia and Suzie, who were young but had proved their mettle and learned enough as apprentices to do simple cuts and weaves under Yaa's watchful eye. Adjoa had also taken on two new apprentices to replace the old ones. One of them was remarkably gifted at microbraids and Senegalese twists, but the other one—who giggled incessantly and had been late for work more than once—showed much less promise.

Through the salon window, Adjoa noticed one of her clients, Cynthia, stepping out of the passenger side of a silver shiny-clean Mercedes. From the first day of business, she'd set a rule that, whenever possible, customers should be greeted before entering the salon. Since the staff and apprentices were busy, Adjoa stepped outside herself to greet Cynthia. It was only once the driver of the car called out "hello" from the front seat that she looked over and recognized the man from Gifty's wedding.

"So we meet again," he said with a smile. "Do you work here?"

Before Adjoa could answer, Cynthia came up next to her and placed her hand on her shoulder. "No, Kwame," she chimed in. "This is Adjoa—she owns the salon."

"Oh, sorry," he said. As Adjoa smiled back to let him know there were no hard feelings, Cynthia introduced the man as Kwame, her younger brother.

"Hello," Adjoa said, seeing a resemblance now. "Thanks for coming—" she started, then said, "That is, for dropping off your sister."

Cynthia asked Kwame to come back for her in an hour, and with a nod in Adjoa's direction he backed the car—too quickly, it seemed to Adjoa—onto Mango Tree Avenue before driving away. As if Cynthia could read Adjoa's mind, she said, "I love my brother, but he drives like a madman. That probably comes from being with cars all day."

Cynthia continued chatting as they walked into the salon, explaining that Kwame had a successful business importing and selling cars. When Adjoa turned her client over to Sylvia for her haircut, Cynthia touched her arm and added, "I thought you'd like to know."

Half an hour later, Gifty and Comfort appeared and were quickly escorted to their seats—Gifty at Yaa's station and Comfort at Adjoa's. One of the apprentices handed them cups of sweetened tea, and the salon staff hovered around Gifty, peppering her with questions about the wedding and her honeymoon in Elmina. As if prompted by their banter, the radio began to play the same Papa Shee song that had played at the wedding.

The name Kwame, Adjoa knew, meant that Cynthia's brother was born on a Saturday, and Saturday-borns tended to be steady and hardworking and willing to go out of their way for others—a good combination of qualities in any man. What kind of hours did someone in Kwame's line of work keep, that he was able to take the time to drop his sister off? Clearly he was a good brother. After another half hour had passed, Adjoa glanced through the salon window every few minutes until she finally spotted Kwame's Mercedes pulling in. She looked at the clock on the wall; he was punctual, too, not on African time at all.

Adjoa asked Suzie to go outside to greet Kwame and sent one of the apprentices to fetch him a cup of tea. Though she tried to focus her attention on Comfort's hair, she couldn't help but notice that, as he entered the salon, Kwame looked around with more interest than the other rare men who stepped inside. Even once he'd been handed a cup of tea, he stood with the cup in his hand, his head making wide arcs as he looked up and down the walls and at every corner of the room.

Adjoa fumbled with her comb and dropped it. She tried to ignore the sharp look that Comfort threw her in the mirror and placed it back in the jar of blue disinfectant on the counter. When she pulled a new comb out of the drawer, the apprentice who'd served Kwame his tea came up to Adjoa to inform her in a low voice that the gentleman was ready to pay his sister's bill.

"Go ahead," said Comfort. "I can wait."

Adjoa placed the comb on the counter and walked behind the front desk where Kwame stood, tapping the desk absent-mindedly with his wallet. "That will be twenty thousand cedis," she said, then added impulsively, "Not many brothers come here to pay for their sisters' hair." There, she'd completed a sentence.

Kwame stopped tapping the desk and leaned toward her. "It was the only way I could think of to talk to you privately," he said, as he flipped open his wallet. "I think I misunderstood at the wedding about whom you left to meet, and I was wondering if we could sit and talk later?"

As he talked, he pulled two 10,000 cedi notes from his wallet with clean, well-manicured hands.

"That would be lovely," Adjoa blurted out, as she took the cedis and placed them in the cash register. She looked to see if the women in the salon had heard her, but Gifty was still regaling Cynthia and the others with stories about her wedding, and no one seemed to be paying attention to

Adjoa's conversation with Kwame—no one, that is, except for Comfort, whose head slowly rotated back to face her mirror after Adjoa caught her eye.

Kwame suggested they meet for lunch on Sunday at Mukaase Restaurant, a place Adjoa had been to once before within the Leisure Centre complex by the airport.

"That would be lovely," she said, irritated that she was repeating herself. Why was she still incapable of saying anything clever?

"Would one o'clock suit you?"

"Yes, that would be . . . fine," she said, stopping herself from using the word *lovely* a third time.

He leaned forward again, "I'm already looking forward to it."

Before she could answer, they were interrupted by Cynthia, inquiring how much she owed for her hairstyle. Sylvia had wound her hair into a thick goddess braid that spiraled upward and around her head, ending in a magnificent peak.

"Kwame's already taken care of it," Adjoa said.

Cynthia placed her hand on her brother's forearm. "You see what a good man he is?"

Kwame shrugged his shoulders, as if to say there was nothing he could do about his sister's embarrassing compliments, but once Cynthia had turned to leave, he said, "See you Sunday, then."

Adjoa smiled and nodded. After the door closed behind them, she took a moment to breathe in the lingering scent of Kwame's cologne, then hurried back to Comfort's chair and grabbed the comb and scissors from the counter.

"Who was that man?" Comfort asked. "He looked familiar. Where have I seen him before?"

"That was Cynthia's brother," Adjoa said.

From the next chair, Gifty chimed in. "Kwame's a friend of Samuel's, Auntie. Didn't you see him at my wedding?"

Comfort turned down the sides of her mouth. "Oh, that's right," she said. "He talked with Ekow about cars. You know he sells used cars from Europe. I've never trusted people in that line of business."

"Auntie, you don't even know Kwame," said Gifty. "I hear he's very kind."

"I didn't say he wasn't," she huffed. "I just said I don't trust people who sell used cars. Those people will sell you a BMW with a Tico motor inside if they can."

"How can you say that?" Gifty said. "Your own son sells cars."

"That's different. He only sells new ones. And only Hondas."

"Well, of course, that's in America. People can afford new cars."

Adjoa paused from cutting Comfort's hair. "Please, can we talk about something besides cars?"

She'd spoken more sharply than she'd meant to, she realized as she felt everyone's eyes on her. Even the apprentices looked up from their work folding freshly washed towels.

But Comfort was nonplussed. "Well, what did this fellow want?"

"Auntie!" Gifty said.

"No, that's fine," Adjoa said. She had no reason not to tell Gifty and Comfort that she planned to meet Kwame for lunch, but it wouldn't do to discuss her private life in front of the salon staff. "I'm used to her questioning, Gifty. Only this time, Auntie, you'll have to let me keep my personal information to myself."

"Then something's cooking between you and Kwame," Gifty said with a smile. "I can't wait to tell Samuel!"

Comfort, however, looked doubtful. "That man is too good-looking. You can never trust a handsome man—they're used to getting whatever they want."

"Where did you ever hear such a ridiculous thing?" said Gifty. "Samuel's handsome, and he's had to work hard for what he has."

Since neither Adjoa nor Comfort jumped in to agree that Gifty's husband was indeed handsome, Yaa broke the silence. "Surely there are *some* handsome men who can be trusted."

But Comfort seemed not to have heard Yaa. "Am I the only one who noticed how he raked over every nook and cranny with his eyes? Be careful, Adjoa. He may be more interested in your money than in you."

Gifty sounded indignant. "Auntie, don't make a fool of yourself. Kwame's already well-to-do. Why shouldn't he take a romantic interest in Adjoa?"

Adjoa wasn't sure what to say. Comfort and Gifty were jumping to conclusions about a budding relationship between her and Kwame, and it was hardly a conversation she wanted to pursue in front of her staff. Still, it was interesting that Comfort had also been struck by Kwame's scrutiny of her salon. Could Comfort be right that he . . . but no, at the wedding Kwame hadn't known she owned a salon, and he'd still asked her to dance. Didn't that prove Comfort's suspicions were unfounded?

"Anyway," Adjoa said out loud, "I've already said we'll be keeping my private life private."

With a knowing glance in the mirror at the apprentices, Comfort nodded her head. "Of course, Adjoa, we don't need to discuss this now. Just keep in mind there's a reason for the expression, 'Before you go into a marriage, ask.'"

"Really," Adjoa started to say, but before she could protest further at the absurdly premature mention of marriage, Comfort raised her hand and added, "I promise I'll say nothing more if you'll just agree to ask around about this fellow."

Gifty jumped in before Adjoa could answer. "But that's easy! He's friends with Samuel. And I can ask Cynthia about him, too. I'll find out what I can, Adjoa, and let you know."

That Sunday after church, Adjoa met Kwame at Mukaase Restaurant. The cloth-covered tables were almost all taken, the restaurant filled with couples and families, some of them still in their church clothes, holding loud conversations.

They both ordered fufu with groundnut soup that was brought out in clay pots. Even though most of the people around them ate their food with their hands, Kwame used his spoon and Adjoa followed his example. Over the noise of people chattering and dishes clanking, he explained about his business and how it allowed him to travel to England or Germany a few times a year. He described the first time he'd driven on the Autobahn, the first time he'd touched snow. At first Adjoa thought he was trying to impress her, but as he continued to talk he just seemed to be trying to make conversation. She enjoyed listening to someone who was intelligent and well-traveled, and the soup had a healthy dose of hot pepper that made it impossible not to savor. By the time they'd finished eating and the server came to clear their empty plates, she was surprised to realize that there were just a handful of customers left in the restaurant.

"I only deal in expensive cars," Kwame was explaining. "They're better quality, so I never have an unsatisfied customer." Adjoa nodded, grateful he hadn't seen her step out of Tony's Tico when she'd been dropped off outside.

"But I've been talking too much about myself and my business," he said, taking a long drink of beer and placing the glass back on the tablecloth. "Tell me about yours. How do you like running the Precious Brother Salon?"

Adjoa thought of Comfort's warning, but Kwame had talked for most of the meal about his own business; it was only natural the conversation would now turn to her salon.

"I like it very much," she said. "It's hard work, but I'm

my own boss. I run the business the way I want to. And my clients seem to like how I run it, because most of them come back."

He nodded. "That's exactly what I like about my busi- ness. I don't have to answer to anyone but myself."

Adjoa took another sip of her Malta soft drink. "Mostly what I enjoy is that I give people a rest from their troubles. When they come to the salon, we take care of them. They can leave their problems behind for a short while, and maybe when they step back outside they feel more refreshed. It's always been my goal that everyone who comes should leave smiling." Adjoa's words surprised her, not what she was say- ing, because it was all true, but the way she was talking so openly with someone she'd just met, as if it were the most natural thing in the world.

Kwame was looking at her thoughtfully. "You seem to be a kind lady."

She clasped her hands and looked out the window at the light traffic on Liberation Avenue heading toward the air- port. During her years in Abidjan, the few times she'd visited home she had gone by bus. Someday, now that she was more comfortable in life, she would like to fly in an airplane—why not to a country like Germany? It was good to have dreams, and even better for them to come true.

"It was always our dream to open a salon, my twin brother and I. Sometimes it still feels unreal, as if I'll wake up one day and be working for someone else again."

"You have a twin?"

Adjoa nodded, pursing her lips. Why had she become so garrulous? She rarely talked about Kojo, and certainly not to people she'd just met.

Kwame seemed not to notice the sudden staunch to Adjoa's flow of words. "I'd like to meet this twin someday. What's his name?"

"Kojo," said Adjoa. As she pronounced her brother's name, a spasm of the familiar arm pain came and went as quickly as it started. "His name was Kojo. He passed away three years ago."

"Oh," he said. "I'm sorry. I'm sure you miss him very much."

"Every day," Adjoa agreed. "We were very close, and even though it's been three and a half years. . . ." She paused.

"I understand," he said. "It takes time, doesn't it? It's been more than four years since I lost my wife."

"Now it's my turn to be sorry," Adjoa said. "I didn't realize you were a widower."

Kwame looked down at his empty glass. "When she died, I didn't think I'd ever meet someone again."

Adjoa fought the urge to reach out and place a comforting hand on his arm, but asked, instead, if they'd had any children. He told her he had two daughters, both of them practically full-grown when they'd lost their mother. One was married now, the other was at university.

"It's very quiet where I live—too quiet," he said, looking at her pointedly. Adjoa didn't lower her eyes from his, letting a comfortable moment of silence linger between them until it was broken by the notes of a cheery song. Kwame pulled a slim mobile from the pocket of his shirt, looked at the screen thoughtfully, and placed the phone back without picking up the call.

"Don't you need to answer that?" asked Adjoa, as the notes continued to play from the pocket of his shirt.

"Right now," Kwame said, "all I need is to talk with you."

For the next week, Kwame called Adjoa every afternoon and they had short, easy conversations, as if they'd already known each other for years. He told her whether he'd sold any cars that day, and about the plans he was making to travel to Germany again. When she recounted the things that had happened during her day—an extra-large tip from a client, the erratic apprentice showing up late for work again, or the announcement from a customer who'd always bragged about her husband that she was getting a divorce—he listened as if she had the most interesting job in the world. It amazed her to think how tongue-tied she'd been the first time she'd met him, and how quickly he'd put her at ease. So natural did it feel to talk with him, in fact, that Adjoa forgot all about Gifty's offer to find out more about Kwame, until she appeared at the salon on Friday morning without an appointment, her face positively shining with excitement.

As she and Adjoa sat down in the armchairs across from the front desk, far from the rest of her staff, Gifty explained in a low, conspiratorial voice that she hadn't learned much from Samuel, who'd met Kwame through another acquaintance.

"You know what men are like," she said, "they never talk to each other about their private lives. But Cynthia had much more to say. Did you know Kwame's a widower with two daughters?"

"Yes, I did," Adjoa said. "He told me on Sunday."

"Cynthia's so pleased he's taken a liking to you. She's tried several times to match him up, but he's never fancied any of them. She'd already given up hope when she talked to him about you. It wasn't until he saw you at the wedding that he seemed to change his mind."

At the mention of the wedding, Adjoa looked up at her friend. "You mean she talked to him about me *before* the wedding? What did she tell him?"

"Just that you owned the salon where she had her hair done and she thought you'd be a good match. Maybe she told him more, I don't know. Why?"

The salon suddenly felt hot and cramped, even though there were only two clients that morning. "Don't you see?" Adjoa said. "That means he knew I owned the salon before he came here. Maybe Comfort was right after all, maybe he—"

But Gifty interrupted. "Kwame is perfect for you, Adjoa! Why are you hesitating? This is your chance to have a family. Why are you letting Comfort's words poison your mind?"

"Because life is hard," Adjoa said, "and this salon is the only thing I have. I can't afford to lose it."

Gifty looked at her friend thoughtfully, and her voice softened. "Adjoa, I know how hard it was to lose Kojo. But remember, bitterness doesn't remain forever in the mouth."

The proper saying, of course, was that sweetness doesn't remain forever in the mouth, but Adjoa didn't correct her friend. Could it indeed go both ways?

"Life is like a mirror," Gifty added, repeating a phrase Adjoa's mother had sometimes used during her childhood. "If you look at it well, it will return the look. Just promise me you'll give him a chance."

Adjoa pondered over Gifty's words all weekend. Her friend was right that she had not been looking in the mirror well when it came to matters of the heart; she ought to give Kwame a chance. Still, she couldn't completely dismiss Comfort's warnings, either, now that she knew he'd been aware of her salon when they met at the wedding. For three nights, she hardly slept, ruminating over her friends' contradictory advice.

On Monday, Kwame dropped by the salon, surprising her with an enormous bouquet of fragrant red roses from an expensive flower shop in Osu. Though Adjoa often bought flowers for the front desk, they were usually simple bouquets of locally available birds-of-paradise, pink hibiscus, or ginger flowers. Kwame's roses, on the other hand, were so massive they took up half the front desk when he placed them there in full view of Adjoa's staff and clients.

"Hello, ladies," Kwame called out to the women who had spun around to stare at him. They nodded at him, beaming, before turning back to their work and conversations as if they hadn't just been gawking. Though the women seemed preoccupied with their own discussions, Adjoa asked Kwame if they might step outside for a moment.

Outside, he told her he'd missed her all week and asked when they could go out again. Despite herself, Adjoa hesitated, her head aching from lack of sleep. Standing next to Kwame's car, she felt a sudden temptation to trace a finger across its shiny surface. Would she pick up a single speck of dirt?

He was looking at Adjoa quizzically. "Don't you want to see me again?" he asked.

Adjoa nodded quickly. "Yes, of course."

"Then why didn't you answer my question just now?"

Adjoa looked in the salon window at the bouquet on her front counter, then back at Kwame. Quickly, before she could stop herself, she blurted out the question that had been burrowing its way through her mind for the last three days, "When you met me at the wedding, Kwame, did you know I owned a salon?"

An odd look flickered across Kwame's face—was it surprise or even anger?—before his features returned to normal. "I'm not sure why you're asking, Adjoa, but I had no idea you owned a salon until Cynthia told me the day I dropped her off. Don't you remember I asked if you worked here? I felt embarrassed about that."

Adjoa felt her stomach sink as he flashed a smile; how could he smile right after telling a lie? "That's not what Cynthia told Gifty," she told him, trying to keep her voice from shaking. "Cynthia said she'd already told you about the salon."

The affable expression on Kwame's face didn't falter. "Gifty must have misunderstood. Yes, Cynthia told me about a woman named Adjoa who ran a salon, but when I saw you at the wedding I didn't know you were the same person. Have you forgotten that we didn't exchange names?"

Adjoa nodded. He was right; she hadn't told him her name.

"It wasn't until my sister introduced you outside the salon that I understood you were the same person."

Of course, it made perfect sense! Adjoa let out a sigh and smiled apologetically at Kwame. "I'm sorry," she said, "I should have realized it before."

But Kwame touched her shoulder. "That's fine, Adjoa. I'm just glad you asked me. People say all sorts of things, and jumping to conclusions can ruin a good relationship. In any case, it's normal to be curious about each other. I've been curious to know more about you, too."

"You have?" Adjoa asked.

"Didn't you notice how closely I looked at the salon the first time I came here? I thought it could tell me more about you than Cynthia or Samuel could."

Adjoa smiled again. Another piece of the puzzle that had been confounding her had clicked into place. His scrutiny of the salon during his first visit finally made sense.

"And?" Adjoa said. "What did it tell you?"

Kwame suddenly looked serious. "I liked what I saw, Adjoa. You're a woman who takes pride in what she does. It's not the fact you own a salon that impressed me—if it was, I'd have let my sister introduce us when she first mentioned you. It was when I saw you at the wedding that I was reminded that in this world we live in pairs."

After Adjoa agreed to meet Kwame again the following Sunday, after he drove off in his shiny car, the rest of the afternoon passed quickly and easily. Even when one of the apprentices broke a bottle of nail polish remover, making the salon smell like alcohol, Adjoa wasn't ruffled. She closed the salon that evening, said good-bye to the staff as they left, and sat down in the armchair by the window, waiting for one of Tony's Ticos to pick her up. As she surveyed the empty parking lot and listened to the steady din of passing traffic, she counted the days until Sunday—five, if you didn't include today. The scent of the roses on the counter wafted in her direction. Why not bring them home with her?

A few minutes later, the Tico pulled up in front of the salon. Tony, who'd been driving her more and more frequently in the past few weeks, stepped out of the driver's side, greeting her as usual with a raised-eyebrows expression.

As he walked around to open her door, his eyes fell on the bouquet she held in her arms, and she noticed a flicker of something pass across his face—a momentary opening of a window that was quickly shut again—before he slipped into his usual pleasant but nondescript expression. To someone who paid little attention to such details, it would have passed unnoticed; but to Adjoa, who made it her job to heed the smallest signs of a person's mood, it was enough for her to suspect something she should have noticed before. It finally made sense that Tony had been picking her up rather than sending his drivers, that he hadn't sent her a bill in nearly two months. The poor man had actually taken a romantic interest in her!

Adjoa looked away, mortified. Though he'd been a godsend when she'd needed his services, and he seemed to be a pleasant and well-intentioned man, she'd never thought of him in that way. She'd just assumed he was married, though a quick glance at his left hand showed it was free of a wedding band. What could he think they had in common? Certainly not enough to have the lively sorts of conversations she had with Kwame. She must at all costs prevent him from being tempted to make an embarrassing declaration of his feelings. Besides, it wasn't fair to let him hope for something when there was no chance.

"I hope you'll find room for these in the backseat," she said, trying to keep her voice light as she handed him the flowers. "They were a gift from my gentleman friend and I couldn't bear to leave them in the salon."

Tony took the vase from her without a word. As she climbed into the car, Adjoa told herself that at some point during the ride she would have to remind Tony again—more firmly than in the past—that he really must send her the late bills for his services.

After their second lunch, Kwame began stopping by the salon every other evening, sometimes taking Adjoa to dinner if she didn't have to work late. She looked forward to seeing him and hearing stories about his day and his plans for expanding his business in the future. He was an excellent listener, too, and always generous with advice, which she appreciated since he was more experienced in matters of business than she was; she'd always suspected her own success with the Precious Brother Salon had been a fortunate accident. When he pointed out how much she was limiting herself by putting all her profits back into the salon and that she could also invest in new ventures, she realized she would have never seen this larger picture. Her thinking had always been limited to the salon.

On the nights Kwame didn't come by, Adjoa called for a car and was relieved that Tony always sent other drivers. When she did see Tony again, two weeks after she'd let him know she was spoken for, it was only to drop Comfort off at the salon.

Adjoa watched from her window and waited for Tony to drive off before she went outside to greet Comfort. Since her friend didn't have an appointment, she asked if she'd come in early for a touch-up.

"No, Adjoa, that's not why I've come," Comfort said. "I've learned something about Kwame I needed to tell you in person. I've been told in the strictest confidence by some-one who's had business dealings with him that he's several million cedis in debt."

Adjoa stared at her friend for several moments, the sound of traffic on Mango Tree Avenue filling the silence between them. The strictest confidence? Several million cedis of debt? What did Comfort have against Kwame that she insisted on making wild allegations against him?

"You know I don't like to meddle, Adjoa," Comfort added, "and I promised not to bring up Kwame again, but he's not to be trusted."

Adjoa wanted to shake Comfort by the shoulders, to tell her to mind her own business and stop spreading rumors when she didn't even know the person she was talking about. How could she stand there, so sure of herself, so unaware of the havoc she was wreaking? She'd always taken an overly keen interest in Adjoa's business, giving unsolicited advice in the early days of the Precious Brother Salon. Back then, Adjoa had tolerated—no, she'd actually welcomed—the old woman's guidance. But this time Comfort had crossed a line. Adjoa had had enough. If Comfort were younger, she would have told her exactly how she felt. Adjoa bit down on her tongue. It wasn't her place to correct her elder, especially since Comfort had been kind to her in the past.

"I can see you need time to take this in," Comfort said. "Tony will be back to pick me up in a few minutes. I'll wait for him here and let you return to your work."

Adjoa knew it was rude not to ask Comfort to wait indoors, but she wasn't feeling particularly gracious, nor did she want to risk Tony coming into the salon. So she walked back inside to her station behind the counter, where she'd been perusing a list of possible investments that Kwame had written down for her the previous night. She stared at the list without really seeing it, tapping at the countertop with a pen.

Comfort's accusation didn't make sense. Cynthia had referred to Kwame as a successful businessman, and there had never been any indication of financial difficulties. Not only did he always pay for their meals as a respectable gentleman would, he didn't seem to hesitate to order the most expensive dishes on the menus, along with imported beers and wines. Besides, she'd already followed Comfort's advice to ask about him, and nothing untoward had bubbled to the surface—to the contrary, Gifty had given her unqualified stamp of approval.

For the first time since Kojo's death, Adjoa had started to finally allow herself to live her life without a constant sense of foreboding, to look into the mirror well, as Gifty had advised. She'd finally started to feel like her old self again— her old self when she and Kojo had first moved to Abidjan, so full of hope. Why was Comfort pushing her back in the direction of forever expecting the worst to happen?

———————

The following Sunday, Kwame took Adjoa back to Mukaase Restaurant, where they sat at the same table, once again eating spicy groundnut soup. They'd arrived later than the usual midday crowd, and only one other table had customers, the waiters sitting bored next to the bar.

As Kwame talked about his upcoming trip to Germany, he was interrupted by the now-familiar ring of his mobile. Adjoa watched as he pulled it from the pocket of his trousers, looked at the number on it, and placed it on the table next to his plate without answering. She felt her stomach drop as the sickening thought came out of nowhere that the call—and all the others he'd ignored when he was with her—were from creditors to whom Kwame owed money. At the same time, she heard Kwame's words replaying in her head from their conversation several weeks ago: jumping to conclusions could ruin a good relationship. She felt so distracted, wondering about the unanswered phone call but not wanting to assume the worst, that she hardly paid attention to the rest of Kwame's discourse.

At end of the meal, when the waiter brought their bill in a small basket and placed it next to Kwame, he reached into his trouser pocket again but came out empty-handed. He patted his other pocket, and even the one on his chest, and then looked over at Adjoa.

"This is terribly embarrassing," he said, "but I seem to have forgotten my wallet. If you wouldn't mind paying for the meal, I'll come by the salon tomorrow and pay you back."

Adjoa willed her hand not to shake as she reached for her purse.

"I'm very embarrassed," Kwame repeated.

Adjoa tried to act naturally, though her fingers fumbled with the cedi notes in her purse. "It's not your fault you forgot your wallet," she said, as she placed the money in the basket. "But it does seem . . . unusual, in light of what someone told me this week."

After a long pause, Kwame asked, his voice unnervingly calm and slow, "What are you talking about?"

Adjoa took a deep breath. "I was told you're several millions of cedis in debt." There, she'd said it.

Kwame's body grew rigid, his hands almost curling into fists. "Who told you that?"

"It doesn't matter who told me," she said, in as calm a manner as she could muster. "What matters is whether it's true."

He stared at her for several moments with narrowed eyes, until his body and hands slowly began to relax.

"Adjoa," he finally said, "you're a businesswoman. I would have thought you of all people would understand. Of course I don't have money in hard cash now; it's all tied up in cars. That's how it works: I borrow money to buy cars, and once I sell them, I pay off the loan and keep the profit. And this meal—these few cedis—are nothing. I've already told you I'll pay you back."

Of course. Once again, Kwame made perfect sense. Why hadn't she thought of that?

"I'm a businessman, Adjoa," he continued, "and though your friends may have unkind things to say about my line of business, I'm doing quite well, thank you."

He held up his hand to keep her from interrupting.

"When I started my business I had next to nothing, but my wife was at my side. All the women I've met since she died turned out to be more interested in my money than in my happiness. When I met you, Adjoa, I thought you were different, but now I can't help but wonder if you aren't the same as the others."

"Goodness, no." Adjoa jumped in.

"Well, how can I know? I'd been thinking I wanted to ask you today to meet my daughters, but now I'm not so sure anymore."

How could she prove to him she was different from the other women who had disappointed him, that she wasn't interested in his money? Adjoa looked at Kwame, at the wounded pride that showed on his face, and blamed herself for having been overly suspicious again, for listening to Comfort's idle chatter. She was relieved when he pushed back his chair and excused himself to go to the gents'.

If only she hadn't let herself be drawn in by Comfort's gossip. But it was too late to rue the past. She had to think fast and figure out what she would say when he came back. Should she appeal to him to understand her own vulnerabilities—that she was in exactly the same position as he was, a businesswoman who had to make sure she was wanted for herself rather than her money? Surely that was something he'd be able to understand.

Adjoa's heart jumped at the sudden happy sound of Kwame's mobile trilling on the table. She looked around and saw that no one seemed to have noticed. As if in a dream, as if a different person momentarily possessed her body, Adjoa watched her hand reach out and pick up the phone. She looked at the screen and saw, simply, the letter *M*. Why just an initial? she wondered, her heart beating even faster. She pressed the TALK button and held the phone to her ear without a word.

On the other end, a woman's voice burst forth. "Hello?" it said. "Hello?"

The voice sounded quite young—most likely one of his daughters. Adjoa answered back, "Hello." What would she ever tell Kwame if he found out she'd answered his phone?

"Who is this?" the voice insisted. "Where is Kwame? I want to speak to him."

"This is Adjoa," she answered, trying to keep her voice even, as if she were taking an appointment at the salon. What kind of daughter referred to her father by his first name? "May I ask to whom I am speaking?"

But the voice sounded angry now. "Who is Adjoa?"

"I'm Kwame's lady friend," she said. "If you'd be so kind as to tell me who you are, I could—"

"*Lady friend*?" the voice interrupted. "I have no idea

what trouble you're trying to stir up, but *I'm* his girlfriend, and you can tell him that I—"

Adjoa lowered the phone from her ear, pressed the OFF button, and dropped it on the table as if it had burned her hand. Glancing toward the men's room to make sure Kwame hadn't come out yet, she pushed back her chair. She forced herself to stand, steadying herself on the back of the chair before she willed her tremulous legs to carry her to the exit. When she finally reached the door and pushed it open, she heard the mobile ringing again, insistently, on the table where she'd left it.

Once she was outside, Adjoa hurried around the corner and called the car service to pick her up. After she hung up, she pictured Kwame returning to their table, wondering if she'd gone to the ladies', and then hearing his phone ring again. Without Adjoa there, he would probably pick it up. She guessed the woman on the other end would keep him talking for a long time. Adjoa began pacing, trying hard not to think about what someone attached to such a young voice might look like. All she wanted was to get back to the salon, to lose herself in the bustle of her customers' lives. Comfort and Gifty had hair appointments later in the week—what would they say if they knew what had just happened? Better not to tell them, or give them some innocuous excuse why she wasn't going to see him anymore—that they'd jointly decided to go their separate ways, perhaps. And Cynthia—what would she say to her? Could she possibly know about her brother's double life or his financial woes? Adjoa doubted it. But it was not her place to meddle in one of her clients' families. For that was what Cynthia was, after all, a client—she was Gifty's friend, not hers. Oh, Gifty, with her horrible advice to look into the mirror well. Just look at how everything went wrong when she'd followed that advice.

Or had she? Adjoa stopped her pacing and looked up at the clear blue sky. Every time Comfort had planted a seed of doubt it had sprouted and thrived in Adjoa's mind like a poisonous weed.

And yet Comfort had been right all along to warn her about Kwame.


When the Tico pulled up ten minutes later, Adjoa was so relieved that it hardly registered when Tony stepped out of the car, the sunlight glinting on his bald head. As he opened the passenger door, he greeted her with his familiar raised-eyebrow glance—as casually as if they'd just seen each other that same morning—and Adjoa finally knew why his expression seemed familiar. Of course: Kojo. Why had it taken her so long to notice? Though they bore no other resemblance, her twin brother had had the exact same habit of raising his eyebrows, an unconscious tic whenever he was about to ask her for something. As Adjoa climbed into the car, it occurred to her that, unlike Kojo, Tony had never asked her for anything. On the contrary, she'd had to plead to pay for his services.

Her door made a dull thud as Tony closed it before he walked to the driver's side, sat down next to her, and started the motor. Only once he'd eased the car onto the street did she realize that she'd been so distracted by what had just transpired with Kwame—and the sudden memory of Kojo—that she hadn't felt the usual tingle of embarrassment at climbing into the funny-looking car. Instead, she settled herself into the seat as if it were the throne of an Ashanti queen. Looking out the car window, Adjoa even attempted a smile. The Tico was not a flashy car, but it was reliable and it would get her where she needed to go.

# Calculations of Risk

Two months after her husband, Peter, quit his job at the Honda dealership, Linda returned home to a state of disarray that had become the norm. Since Peter was there most of the day except for his evening classes, they had withdrawn eight-year-old Amanda and six-year-old Noah from their after-school program, and the house seemed to transform itself overnight into a magnet for the other children of the neighborhood. They left traces of the day's activities in every room like telltale crumbs: a Sorry! board on the dining room table with its dice and tokens strewn underneath, Mr. Potato Head pieces littered on the living room carpet, red plastic monkeys that escaped from their barrel to scatter across the kitchen floor.

At first, the mess infuriated her. She had several arguments with Peter, who said the children couldn't help it, and she'd tried imposing strict rules that they had to clean up before dinner. Part of her frustration, Linda knew, was due to the fact that instead of consulting her about leaving his job, Peter had simply announced one Sunday evening that he'd quit work the previous Friday. He claimed he'd been overlooked for a promotion either because he was black or because he was from Ghana or both. He planned to focus on finishing up his master's degree in economics so he could get a proper job, as he called it, when he graduated in five months. He'd been right to be upset, of course, but Linda couldn't help worrying how they'd make ends meet with just her salary as an actuary with an insurance company in downtown Washington, D.C.

After several weeks of trying to impose order on the chaos of their house, Linda grew tired of being the only one who seemed to care that they lived in a sty. She decided to stop worrying that someone might trip on something, figuring that if they were lucky there would be nothing more than tears, possibly a scraped knee, and then, maybe then, they would finally listen.

Today, she found Amanda and Noah bent over a stack of pickup sticks, Amanda's old dress-up costumes strewn around them. She kissed each of them on their heads, brushing her lips against their soft curls.

"Hi, Mom," they muttered, focused on their game.

"Where's Daddy?"

Amanda tilted her head in the direction of the study, a closed-in porch they'd turned into an extra room. She bent her long and graceful neck with an uncanny adult elegance—a gesture that didn't come from Linda's side of the family. Though both of her children were attractive, with their black corkscrew curls and honey-colored skin, she could already tell that Amanda was going to be stunning. She'd noticed more than once the eyes of grown men, both white and black, lingering on her daughter's hair, and every time it had made her stomach flip like a landed fish.

With a last glance at the top of her children's heads, Linda went into the study and found Peter at his desk, staring at a computer monitor. At his feet, one of the neighborhood children, Marvin, sat bent over a sheet of paper, drawing on it with a pencil. The only son of the only African-American family on their block, Marvin was a known fixture in the neighborhood, a big and loping thirteen-year-old whose mind hadn't developed along with his body. Linda had seen him occasionally in the nearby park and learned from another parent that he went to a special school.

Neither Peter nor Marvin heard Linda walk in, their attention focused on their respective tasks, both of them hunched over with the same arc in their backs. It occurred to Linda that to someone who didn't know their family, Marvin looked more like Peter's son than Noah did.

"Hi, Peter," she called out. "Hi, Marvin." They both looked up. "Have a good day?" she asked Peter.

He flashed his lopsided smile, the kind he used to give her early in their relationship when she'd frame his face with her hands, marveling at the contrast of his smooth dark skin against her pale pink hands. When was the last time in their nine-year marriage that she had reached out to hold his face?

"Brilliant," he said. "I finally figured out how my thesis is going to fit together."

"Great," she said. "You can tell me about it over dinner. Marvin, it's near dinnertime. Your mother's probably looking for you."

Marvin looked up at Peter, who gave him a slight nod. "Yeah," said the boy, his voice disconcertingly deep as he raised himself up from the floor. "My mom's probably looking for me."

Even though he slouched in his hooded sweatshirt and baggy jeans, he was several inches taller than Linda. Without looking at her, he added, as if it were a natural segue from his previous comment, "Mom might buy me a dog."

Linda reminded herself to be patient. He was like a young child, after all. "That's nice, Marvin."

"Well, see you," he said to Peter, before he shuffled out of the study. She followed him to the front door.

"Say hi to your mother for me, okay?" she told him. "Will you remember to tell her Linda said hi?"

"Sure," Marvin said, jamming his hands into his pockets and turning to amble down the steps of the front stoop.

Inside, Peter was pouring himself a beer in the kitchen. "Want some?" he asked. When she nodded, he reached for a second glass and poured the rest of his bottle into it.

She took a sip before placing the glass back on the counter. "Does Marvin come here every day?"

"Most days," he said. "Sometimes he plays with the others, sometimes he just hangs around with me. Let's face it, he doesn't quite fit in with them."

Linda nodded. "What do you two talk about?"

"Nothing much. Usually I work and he just mucks around."

It was not hard for Linda to imagine that Marvin, who lived with his mother and two sisters, had found a father figure in Peter. She felt a warmness, a surge of pride that someone would seek him out in that role. He had a way with children—not just their own but other people's as well. He was neither standoffish nor overly intent on befriending them—mistakes she saw other adults make, including herself.

"I don't know how you manage to stay so calm amid the chaos," she said, "and get work done for your classes."

Peter flashed his crooked smile again. "It reminds me of my childhood," he said. "I'd be studying while my younger brothers and sisters were running about and creating a fuss. I suppose I got used to it. Besides, you know what it's like in Accra—there's always a child underfoot or a baby being thrust into your arms."

They had visited Ghana four years ago, after saving up to go as a family so that Amanda and Noah could meet their African relatives. The children adapted well and Linda tried to enjoy herself for Peter's sake. But at most of the gatherings they attended, she was the only white person, making her feel self-conscious. It didn't help that Peter's family, who called him by his other name, Ekow, spoke mostly in Fante. She hated not knowing what people were saying and suspected they were talking about her, commenting on how she didn't take to the local food, refused to dance to African music, or wouldn't let the children out of her sight.

When she'd first met Peter at college in the Northeast, she'd conveniently ignored the fact that he came from a different culture. It was easy enough to do when they were far away from their families—hers in a small town in Minnesota. During college, and even when they lived together before getting married, Peter had seemed to want to be and do everything American. It wasn't until after the children were born that he began to assert his Ghanaian culture.

Their relationship had surprised everyone, including herself. She knew going into the marriage how risk averse she was. Marrying someone from a foreign culture was possibly the biggest gamble she would make in her life. Only later did she understand she'd sought out someone as different as possible from the frat boys she'd hung around with her freshman year—rich white boys who stalked the campus in packs like wolves. Peter seemed like their polar opposite: dead serious about his studies, his accent formal and polite. And though she was less sure why he'd fallen in love with her, and wondered sometimes whether he'd considered it a gamble as well, even in their most difficult periods she refused to believe her parents' accusation that he'd married her to become an American citizen.

Peter was looking at her. "You seem tired," he said,

reaching for her with both arms and pulling her toward him. "Don't worry, things will get better. Once I finish my degree and get a good job, then, if you want, *you* can take time off and stay home with the children."

She sighed. No matter how many times she'd gone over their finances with him, he still didn't get it—they needed the double income to keep living in the moderately upscale suburb where they'd moved right before Amanda was born, not to mention saving for the kids' college funds. Besides, she had to admit the idea of staying home with a herd of children didn't tantalize her. When Amanda and Noah were babies, she'd had a hard time tearing herself away from them, anxious about all the things that could go wrong. At night, she'd hardly slept, checking on them every hour because she was terrified they'd simply stop breathing, victims of sudden infant death syndrome. But now that they'd grown into healthy, robust children, she found she preferred the quiet of her office, poring over statistics, calculating every conceivable risk, building safety nets for all the things that could go wrong in a dangerous world.

Several weeks later, Linda walked the five blocks home from the bus stop, her medium-high heels clicking against the pavement, the weight of her laptop bearing down on her shoulder. It was a cool, early spring evening, the sun just beginning to set. Because there were no sidewalks, and both sides of the streets were lined with parked cars, she walked in the middle of the street. When she heard a car coming up behind her, she moved to the side, slipping between two SUVs until the car passed.

Up ahead, three boys leaned against a car that didn't belong there—a beat-up hatchback with fading red paint. They jostled each other and made whooping sounds. In the darkening light of the early evening, the kids looked about sixteen, two of them white, one black, all dressed in the teen-age uniform of baggy jeans and oversized sweatshirts. She didn't recognize them; they were older than the children on her block, most of whom, with the exception of Marvin, were still primary-school age. At the thought of Marvin, Linda stopped in her tracks—it was him, she realized, with the two older boys.

The boys hadn't shown any sign of noticing her, and she continued walking down the middle of the street. As she neared them, they stopped laughing and muttered in low voices. A cigarette dangled in one of the older boys' hands, smoke drifting from his mouth.

Once she'd come within ten feet of them, she called out, trying to sound casual, "Hello, Marvin."

But Marvin, staring intently at the smoke floating from the other boy's cigarette, seemed not to have heard her, while the two other boys turned and stared.

She wanted to stop, grab Marvin by the shoulder, and repeat his name. What was wrong with these kids? She was near enough to smell them—a mix of body odor, cigarette smoke, and something else, possibly alcohol. She felt the older two boys' eyes inch up and down her body, and her instincts urged her to move on, to get home before the sky turned any darker, so she walked past them, her heart beating faster than her footsteps as she willed herself not to run. She felt the back of her neck grow rigid under their real or imagined gaze—she didn't want to let them see her turn around to look at them, so she didn't know which. Another car length and she'd be there. Then her heels clacked along the flagstone walkway up to her front stoop. She let herself leap up the final step before she threw open the front door, glad for once that Peter always left it unlocked when he was home. When she glanced back, the two older kids were climbing into the car they'd been leaning against, while Marvin waved at them side-to-side like a child.

Linda waited till the children were asleep and she was alone in bed with Peter before she told him about Marvin and his two friends.

"Did they say something to you or touch you?" he asked. His voice was sharp, protective, and Linda felt the warmth of his body against hers under the covers. This was the Peter she remembered from college, the one who always made her feel safe.

"No," she said, "nothing like that. It just made me uneasy. Those kids aren't from this neighborhood. Was Marvin here today?"

"He stopped by after school, but then he said he was meeting friends at the park and rode off on his bike."

It didn't add much to what she already knew, other than the unsettling fact that Marvin considered those boys his friends. "The whole thing just makes me uneasy," she repeated.

"I know him, Linda," Peter said. "He's a good kid."

"I didn't say he wasn't a good kid," Linda said. "It's just that a boy that's . . . well, like *him*, is so impressionable. I don't think he should hang around older boys like those two. Maybe you could talk to him. Find out how he knows them, what they do together."

"If it'll make you feel better," he said, "I'll talk to him."

"It *would* make me feel better," Linda said, then added, "Please."

After Peter switched off the light on the nightstand, Linda kept her eyes open, watching the furniture in their room begin to take shape as her eyes adjusted to the darkness. She sighed; she knew she wouldn't be able to fall asleep quickly. She turned to pull Peter's arm around her, and he drew her tightly against him, just as he had the first night they'd spent together. How her heart had rushed toward the feeling of safety that night, how well she'd slept.

With Peter, Linda had finally been able to let go of what had happened during her freshman year with Tyler, the frat boy she'd worshipped for months who'd invited her to his dorm room one night. Not that the memories—patchy as they were after too much beer and tequila—ever fully went away. The Beastie Boys shouting from the stereo, the smell of cigarettes on his hand as he covered her mouth, the dead weight of his body on top of her struggling one. She'd thought of reporting what had happened to the school administrators, but wasn't she to blame, too, for going to his room, for drinking so much she'd been unable to fight him off? Better to learn her lesson well and never forget it: the world was a dangerous place, and she could never be too vigilant in keeping herself and the people she loved out of harm's way. She never told anyone what had happened, not even Peter when they started dating two years later. What if he had tried to hurt Tyler and possibly been harmed himself—or even arrested?

But even without Peter knowing what had happened, Linda felt he had saved her. Once they'd started dating, she was able to keep her fear at bay—to become careful rather than fearful, vigilant rather than paranoid. Now, lying in bed and listening to his deep breathing ease into a low snore, thinking about Marvin and the badly behaved teenagers, she wondered whether she'd been fooling herself all this time.


The day of Peter's graduation, the family stopped on their way home for his favorite treat of Vietnamese *pho* soup. While the children built a log cabin with plastic chopsticks from the lazy Susan on their table, Peter told her he'd applied online to a job posting he'd shown her that weekend. He looked so happy and handsome in his black gown, unzipped to show his suit underneath, that Linda didn't have the heart to point out that the position required management experience—something he didn't have.

Later, when Peter pulled the car up in front of their house, Marvin was sitting on the stoop, his elbows on his knees and his chin propped in his hands. In the several weeks since she'd run into him with the two older boys, she hadn't seen him again, and neither Peter nor the children had mentioned him. She'd assumed he spent his time with his older friends now, so he neatly, imperceptibly slipped off her radar screen.

"My mom's getting her hair done," he informed them, as they walked up the flagstone path. "I didn't want to go with her so she said I should come here. Why are you wearing that dress?" he asked Peter.

"It's my graduation robe. I got my master's degree today."

"That's nice," Marvin said. "Did I tell you I picked out the dog I want?"

Peter shook his head, while Noah asked, "What dog are you getting, Marvin?"

"It's going to be a pit bull."

"A pit bull?" Linda said. "Why would you want to get such a mean dog?"

"My friends told me," he said.

"Told you what?" she asked. But he only looked at her blankly.

"And your mother's finally agreed to get you the dog?" asked Peter.

"She said she'd think about it." He looked at Peter. "Do you think you can talk to her?"

Peter reached out and patted him on the shoulder. "If she said she's thinking about it, I'm sure she's giving it all her attention." He unlocked the front door and the children went inside, with Marvin following them.

Linda stood on the stoop, looking up at Peter.

"Did you ever talk to him?" she asked. "Did you ask him about those boys I saw with him?"

Peter nodded. "I did, actually. He said he spends time every now and then with some kids he met at the park."

"But he still comes here?"

"Not as often as before," Peter said. "Just a few times a week."

"Why didn't you tell me?" she asked.

"You had a problem with his friends, Linda, not with him. Besides, you didn't ask about it anymore."

Linda looked at Peter. Even though he was right—rather than assuming that Marvin no longer came, she should have asked—she couldn't help feeling that he'd been hiding something from her. With the faintest shake of his head, Peter turned and walked into the house.

Watching her husband's retreating back, Linda wondered if she was being too hard on Marvin. Had her own demons gotten in the way of assessing the situation objectively, something she had no problem doing at work when it concerned people she didn't know? Peter was right that her problem wasn't with Marvin but with his friends. Still, couldn't a boy as impressionable as Marvin be talked into doing things a normal child would know was wrong? Or was it his mental handicap, his simplemindedness—however she was supposed to refer to his mild case of retardation—that she feared, as if it might rub off on one of the kids, when in fact being around him might just teach them to be compassionate? The sound of laughter erupted from the living room. Along with Amanda and Noah's high-pitched giggles, Linda made out a strange snorting sound that clearly belonged to Marvin— the kind of laugh other kids jeered at.

In any case, once Peter got a job the children would go back to after-school care, and Marvin's mother would have to palm him off on some other neighbor.


But summer came and went, and despite several interviews, Peter still hadn't found work. Apparently, no one needed economists anymore. During the summer months, Linda forced herself to be patient; she knew it took time to find a job, and besides with Peter home they didn't have to pay for daycare while the children were on vacation. This was surely just another temporary bump on the road she'd chosen when she'd married Peter, like the challenging four months when her meddlesome and controlling mother-in-law, with the improbable name of Comfort, had stayed with them after Amanda's birth. Even her parents' two-year silence, following their boycott of her wedding, had been temporary, finally giving way to terse phone calls about their grandchildren that eventually thawed out relations enough for annual holiday visits.

But once Amanda and Noah were back in school, Linda began to feel on edge again. They weren't in enough of a financial bind to panic yet, but over the last three months they'd started accruing credit card debt on top of the mortgage and Peter's school loans, never mind following their original plan to tuck away money for the kids' college fund. Peter needed to earn money—at this point she didn't care how. When she suggested in September that he get a part-time job while the children were at school, he agreed to look into it but then declared he was overqualified for all the part-time work he'd come across.

"Just get something until you get your dream job," she told him. "Just to keep you busy and have a bit of cash flowing in."

But he was surprisingly stubborn. "That's what I did at the car dealership—and you saw what a trap that was. I spent ten years in a job I hated. I'm not doing that again."

In the meantime, Linda tried not to begrudge the fact that she continued to work full days as the sole family provider. Still, she could feel her resentment overshadow the pleasure she used to take in her work. When she came home, no one asked her how her day had been, no one acknowledged the endless slog her life had become. She tried to sleep in on weekends, to recharge her batteries for the next week, but she woke up early anyway, while Peter had no difficulty sleeping well into the morning.

One Saturday morning in early November, Linda woke up to a gleam of sunlight leaking into the bedroom between the curtains. She stood up and pulled the curtain to the side, revealing a cloudless, Windex-blue sky. Peter hadn't stirred in their bed, and she opened the window a notch, letting a light breeze blow inside and replace the stale indoor air. For the first time in weeks, the sound of the children playing in their room made her smile rather than feel over-come with fatigue, made her feel that the sacrifices she had made—was continuing to make—were all worthwhile.

"How about pancakes this morning?" she asked, and Amanda and Noah answered with enthusiastic shouts.

After they'd gorged themselves on pancakes, Linda looked at the sticky plates on the table and the dirty bowl and fry-ing pan in the sink. She could wash up, or she could take advantage of the beautiful weather and take the children for a walk along the creek several blocks from their house. For once, she was going to seize the moment.

Outside, the temperature was perfect—a classic Indian-summer day. Amanda walked ahead of them, while Noah held Linda's hand as they reached the woods. In the shade of the tall trees, Noah let go and sprinted to the edge of the creek, where he squatted on a stone, holding a stick and pretending to fish.

Meanwhile, Amanda had leaped to the other side of the creek, where she scanned the ground and picked something up. "Look what I found!" she shouted, holding up a stone that glinted for a second before she slipped it into the pocket of her jeans. Probably another piece of mica, one that would have disintegrated into flecks by the time Linda emptied Amanda's pockets to do the laundry.

In the distance, Linda heard voices, more raucous than usual for these woods. They grew louder as their source appeared—a group of five kids, Marvin among them, as well as the two boys from last spring, one of them wearing a black T-shirt emblazoned with the image of a skull.

From across the creek, Amanda called out, "Hi, Marvin."

Noah looked up and added, "Hey, Marvin!"

The boys began to imitate Amanda and Noah's high-pitched voices, "Hi, Marvin," "Hey, Marvin," and Marvin chortled, making the same snorting sounds Linda had noticed when he'd laughed in her home.

"What's so funny?" Linda asked.

"'What's so funny?'" the boys repeated. They stopped in front of Linda and looked at her, jostling each other and repeating her words in falsetto voices. "What's so funny?"

"Marvin." Linda tried to make her voice sound authoritative.

But Marvin's eyes were on the apparent ringleader, the

boy with the skull T-shirt, who said, "Hey, lady, you know Marvin?"

"Of course I do," she said. "He's our neighbor. He plays with my children."

"He's our lucky charm, aren't you, Marvin?"

Marvin nodded, letting out a single, nervous snort. "Marvin, you play with those kids?" the ringleader asked.

"Yeah, sure I do," he answered.

"That pretty girl over there?" the boy asked. "You play with her?"

Marvin looked at Amanda. "Yeah, that's Amanda."

Skull Boy grinned, his pale lips parting to show already yellowing teeth. "Amaaaanda," he repeated, then made a smacking sound with his lips. "Next time, Marvin, you let me play with her, too, okay?"

Linda took a step forward, adrenaline pumping. This is crazy, she thought. These are children, not men. Where did they learn to behave this way, to make lewd innuendos and threatening comments? What would they be capable of in a few years if no one reined them in?

"Who are you kids?" she said, her voice sounding more shrill than she intended. "Do you live around here? Who are your parents?"

The boys fell silent and looked at each other with questioning glances until the ringleader answered, "I don't have any parents, how about that?" And then all of them, even Marvin, started their grating laughter again.

Linda felt Amanda and Noah watching her as she tried

to assess the situation. What was the likelihood of this pack of boys giving in to their surging testosterone and attacking them? Ten percent? Twenty-five? Fifty? When an image flashed before her eyes of the kid in the T-shirt raising his hand to grab Amanda, she pulled herself together.

"Kids," she said to Amanda and Noah, "we're done playing. Let's go home." She turned and looked directly at Marvin. "Marvin, I'll be stopping by your mother's house this afternoon to say hi."

She knew it wasn't much; these boys would hardly care if she talked to Marvin's mother. But she wanted to remind them that they were all children and she the adult. She grabbed Noah's hand and Amanda crossed the creek, prompting the ringleader to repeat her name in a singsong litany, though Amanda had the good sense not to look at him. Linda placed one arm around each of her children's shoulders to lead them in the opposite direction from which the boys had been walking. She felt the faintest trembling in Amanda's shoulder—or was it her own hand?—as she shepherded her children away. Only Noah turned around and waved. "Bye, Marvin," he said.

"Bye-bye."

She heard Marvin's voice behind her, and despite herself she picked up her pace as the other boys started laughing again, falling into a litany of high-pitched, mocking *Bye-byes* that nearly drowned out the ringleader's voice as he called out, "See you around, Amaaaanda."

Even though she could tell from the receding sound of

the boys' laughter that they weren't being followed, Linda continued to walk at a swift pace.

"You're walking too fast, Mom," Noah whined.

"Why don't you run ahead a bit, Noah? Get some exercise." She watched as he sprinted a few yards ahead. "But not too far," she called out.

"What was wrong with those guys, Mom?" Amanda asked.

"I don't know," Linda answered, "but if anyone ever talks to you like that, you need to get away from them as fast as possible. And you need to tell me about it. Do you understand?"

Her daughter's dark eyes locked with hers. "I understand," Amanda said. Then she added, "Those boys were mean, Mom, but Marvin's not mean. He's not smart, but he's nice."

"He just doesn't know any better," Linda said. "Sometimes people don't act like themselves when they're with the wrong people."

When they returned home, they found Peter in the kitchen, standing next to the counter, drinking coffee, surrounded by the dirty dishes they'd left after breakfast.

"Amanda, Noah, why don't you go outside and play on the swing set?" she said to the children.

"Daddy, will you come push me?" asked Noah, tugging at the hem of his father's shirt.

Peter smiled down at his son and tousled his hair. "Sure," he said, placing his mug on the counter. "Sounds like fun."

But Linda touched Peter's arm and whispered, "I need to talk to you."

Peter nodded. "You go ahead, Noah," he said, holding the back door open for the children to scamper out. "I'll be right out," he called after them before he turned to face Linda.

"I'd say let's sit down at the kitchen table," he said, "but as you can see it's a mess."

"We were in a hurry to get outside this morning."

"You complain every day what a mess the house is, and then you do this? You left it for me to clean up, didn't you?"

Linda paused. She hadn't actually planned it like Peter claimed, but now that he'd brought it up, what would be so wrong with him cleaning it up? He didn't have a job, for God's sake, he had lots of free time. Would it kill him to pitch in more around the house?

Peter was staring at her. "Do you have any idea how hard things are for me right now?" he said. "Where I come from, a man isn't a man unless he provides for his family. Expecting me to be the cleaning service is just an added humiliation."

She looked at him, standing tall and rigid against the kitchen counter. Hard for *him*? So now she had to be understanding of how hard things were for *him*? What about her? He never asked how *she* was doing, never seemed to be there when she needed him. Not even today, in the woods.

She buried her head in her hands. "Oh, God, Peter, this isn't the conversation we need to have right now. We were almost attacked in the woods just now, me and the children."

"What? What happened?" She felt his hands touching her arm.

"It was Marvin and those boys," she said, lowering her hands and leaning against his chest. "There were five of them this time. They made comments . . . about Amanda."

"Marvin?" His torso stiffened against hers. "Are you sure they wanted to hurt you, Linda? I mean, I don't know about the other kids, but Marvin—"

Linda pulled away. "Yes, Peter, I'm sure." She turned to the kitchen table and began to stack the dirty dishes, their sharp clatter strangely reassuring. "And another thing I'm sure of is that I don't want that boy in this house again. I don't want him near Amanda, or Noah for that matter."

"Linda, that's too drastic. Let's talk this through."

But Linda shook her head as she carried the stack of plates to the sink. "No, Peter. The only talking we need to do is with his mother. She needs to know what kind of kids her son is hanging out with."

From outside, Noah's voice called out for his father.

"Go," she said. "I'll finish up here."

In the afternoon, after Peter dropped Amanda and Noah at a play date, they walked to Marvin's house. One of his sisters opened the door for them, letting them know her mother was home but Marvin was not. She led them to the living room, furnished with overstuffed velvet armchairs and a matching sofa that looked like they'd once been burgundy-colored and had faded into a dusty pink. On the wall, prints of watercolor landscapes were framed in cheap metal frames. In the corner, Linda noticed a yellow oversized stuffed dog with floppy ears and a red felt tongue—probably an attempt to appease Marvin's requests for a dog.

Marvin's mother offered them coffee, which Linda declined and Peter accepted. Once she'd brought Peter's mug of coffee, she sat down across from them as Linda explained the reason for their visit. "We've come to talk to you about Marvin. This isn't easy, but I think you should know that he's made friends with some older boys who are trouble. I ran into them in the woods this morning, and they practically threatened to hurt my daughter."

"Friends? What friends?" she asked. "The only kids he talks about are your children and the other children that come to your house. And he talks about you, Peter. I assume that when he's not here, he's with you."

Peter remained silent, fidgeting with his mug, pushing it around the coffee table, so Linda jumped in. "Well, not all the time," she explained. "I ran across him and two of these boys several months ago, and this morning there were five of them in the woods."

"What did he say?" she asked. "What exactly did my son say?"

Linda looked at the stuffed dog in the corner before she forced herself to face the woman. "He didn't say anything, really," she admitted. "It was the other boys, saying they wanted to play with my daughter, and saying it in a lewd way."

Marvin's mother stiffened, her posture impeccably erect. "I'm sorry for what those boys may have said to you or your daughter, but before I reprimand my son I need you to tell me exactly what he did wrong."

Linda had to admit that he hadn't, in fact, done anything wrong. "But I think you should know he's running with the wrong crowd. If it were my son, I'd want to know. He just seems so impressionable, like they could talk him into doing something he wouldn't normally do. And peer pressure can be so strong, you know, just to be one of the boys."

Marvin's mother looked at Linda appraisingly for several seconds before turning to Peter and asking him what he thought.

He cleared his throat before answering. "I don't know what to think. I wasn't there and I've never seen those kids."

Linda looked over at Peter, too surprised to speak. Even though she'd known him most of her adult life and had borne him two children, even though he was sitting right next to her on the couch, she felt as if she were looking at a stranger on the other side of the widest river in the world.

They walked home in silence, but once they were back in the house, Linda lit into him. "Why didn't you help me out? Why did you make me look like I was overreacting?"

"I just told the truth."

"Are you saying I lied? Are you saying that situation in the woods today wasn't dangerous?"

Peter spoke slowly. "I'm not saying you don't believe it was dangerous. But I can't imagine that poor boy wanting to harm anyone."

"I never said he *wants* to harm anyone. All I'm saying is he has the physical strength to hurt one of my children, and who knows what one of those kids could put him up to? You didn't see him with those older boys, Peter. He's too impressionable and weak-minded to think for himself."

"You keep saying that, but are you sure it's just that he's impressionable?" he asked in a flat voice.

Linda hesitated, unmoored by the fact that their conversation had drifted in an unknown direction. "What are you saying?"

"Come on now, Linda. You know what I mean."

"No, really," she said. "Tell me, Peter."

Peter swallowed. "Are you sure you're not looking at him differently because of the color of his skin?"

"What? God, Peter, you can't just pull the race card every time you want things to go your way. Why don't you just see things for what they are? That boy isn't *normal*."

Peter's eyes bored into hers. "Just tell me one thing: the boys he was with—were they white or black?"

Linda hesitated for a moment, her heart pounding as if she were about to walk into a trap. But when she realized it was Peter who had misstepped, her anger returned. "I don't see what that has to do with it, but since you seem to think it's so damned important, they were white, Peter, okay? Every single one of them was as white as *this*." She pointed with her finger at the skin on her cheek and then spun around to leave.

"Linda," he said, grabbing her arm. "Wait!"

"Don't touch me," she yelled.

He dropped her arm, raising both hands in surrender. "Calm down, Linda. There's no reason to shout. I'm sorry, okay?"

"Jesus, Peter. You just accused me of being racist!"

"Oh, hell," he said. "Linda, it's this bloody country. Before I came here, I never paid attention to black or white, I didn't care. I thought if I closed my eyes to it, it wouldn't affect me. But look what happened at the dealership. It's real, Linda. Racism is as real for me as it will be for Amanda and Noah."

Linda took in a deep breath; she refused to be diverted. "I just want our children to be safe, Peter, and I know that's what you want, too. I don't care if those boys are white or black or purple, they threatened Amanda and I don't want them putting Marvin up to anything. The safest thing is not to let Marvin come over here anymore."

"He's just a kid, Linda. Noah and Amanda are friends with him; how do we explain to them that he's banned from the house? Listen, I promise when he's here I'll keep a close eye on him. I won't leave him alone with the kids. Would that satisfy you?"

Linda racked her brain for any reason she could give—

reasons that made it unequivocally clear that the color of Marvin's skin was not an issue—but couldn't think of anything else to say. No matter how he'd breached her trust as a husband by not backing her up at Marvin's house, she couldn't dispute that he was a good and caring father and she could trust him to watch over their children. Still, she hesitated.

Peter continued. "If what you're saying is true, if those boys really do have that kind of influence over him, the best thing for him is to spend time here and away from them."

There was a logic to this, though she refrained from pointing out that last she'd checked they weren't running a social agency out of their home.

Defeated, she finally relented. "Okay, if you promise never to leave them alone with him, he can keep coming over."

"Good," said Peter. "You won't regret it. Besides, it won't be for long. I'll find a job soon, I promise."

It was all Linda could do to hold her tongue. Sure, that was going to happen real soon.


True to his word, within a month Peter secured a job at a think tank, explaining that it wasn't exactly what he'd been looking for, but the organization seemed solid and he could work his way up. The children began their after-school program, and most days Linda picked them up after work since Peter was working late to prove himself to his new boss.

Linda was grateful that they finally had a double income again, so they could start chipping away at the debt that had mounted over the last ten months. The family was busier than ever, the fall and winter slipping past at a surreal pace as the children made new friends and no longer talked about Marvin. She hired a cleaning lady to come on Wednesdays and relished coming home on cleaning day, anticipating the smell of air freshener, the sparkling bathroom, the tracks left by the vacuum cleaner on the downstairs carpet. Along with the new and welcome tidiness of their house, Linda embraced the order of the family's daily schedule. From the shrill ring of the alarm clock to the children's good-night story, their time was as programmed and predictable as possible with two young children in the house.

Whenever she thought back on the eight months that Peter was unemployed, she saw it as a test that she'd passed by her own wits and determination. She'd been able to support her family on her own; she'd stood up to the boys in the woods; she and Peter and the kids had survived. Whatever other bad things awaited them, they were most likely things she couldn't anticipate. Worrying was as ineffective as her long-ago nighttime crib checks to see if her babies were still breathing.

The following spring, on a Sunday morning when the children were away at a play date, Linda sat upstairs folding laundry in her bedroom while Peter worked on the computer downstairs. She pulled a warm towel from the hamper and held it up to her nose, inhaling the freshly washed smell, as she glanced out the window across the newly mown lawns of the neighborhood. Down the street, Marvin was playing on his front lawn with a dog. She stood up and walked toward the window for a better look. The dog was pint-sized, a gray-haired mutt that looked nothing like a pit bull. Marvin sat cross-legged in the middle of the lawn, the animal frolicking around him and darting in for periodic playful attacks before running away again. He was inordinately gentle, letting the dog nip at him as if he didn't feel a thing.

At the sight of Marvin's gentleness, Linda felt a wave of guilt. After all, she had tried to keep him from her family. She ought to go out and say "Hi," maybe admire and pet the dog. But there was another load of laundry waiting, and she still needed to fit in a trip to the grocery store before she picked up the kids in an hour.

Outside, Marvin put the dog on a leash and crossed the street toward their house, the dog trotting next to him. A few seconds later, the doorbell rang.

"Can you get that?" she shouted to Peter.

Linda heard them downstairs, the sound of two men having a conversation, but couldn't make out what they were saying. Within minutes, she heard the door slam and watched Peter walking with Marvin down the flagstone path, his arm around the boy's shoulder as they crossed to the other side of the street, the puppy in Marvin's arms. Linda could make out Peter's amiable lopsided grin as he bent forward to scratch the dog behind its ears. Then Marvin, too, leaned forward and their foreheads touched, converging into a simple, perfect arc.

# There Are No Accidents

As the driver inched the car through lunch hour traffic near Sankara Circle, Janice sat in the passenger seat and watched a young girl—just a few years older than Janice's six-year-old daughter, Alemnesh— darting between cars with a tray of red-ripe mangoes balanced on her head. A woman called out from a bus, and the girl rushed over, holding the tray up to the window for her to pick out two mangoes. When the bus jolted forward, the woman tossed a coin from the window, and Janice caught her breath as the girl ducked behind a taxi in the direction of the coin's trajectory. Two seconds later, she exhaled at the sight of the child resurfacing, clutching the tray with both hands, holding the mangoes against her chest as she scurried away and slipped out of Janice's sight.

Alemnesh, thank God, was safely tucked away in school, learning to add and subtract rather than dodging traffic. Janice absentmindedly watched people milling on the broad sidewalk or standing in front of the shops. Though it had

been a difficult three months as Alemnesh adjusted to their
new environment, they seemed to be over the worst of it.
Still, Janice wondered whether she'd done the right thing
by moving them from Senegal to Ghana. Not that she'd
had lots of choices. Her job had finally come to an end, and
the only other offers had been for countries that were less
stable, places like Chad that were out of the question with a
small child. She was doing the best she could, she reassured
herself, as they inched down a new block, passing a shop
painted baby-pink before she realized that they'd just passed
a familiar face. How could that be—here in Accra, where
she knew only a handful of people? But that round face and
serious expression, the neatly pulled-back hair—it had to
be Adjoa, her Ghanaian masseuse when she'd lived in Abidjan. Janice glanced at her watch—they'd factored in more
than enough time for traffic; they would probably even be
early for her meeting at the Ministry of Health. On an
impulse, she asked the driver to pull over. He steered the car
to the side of the road, and she jumped out and sprinted over
to the woman.

"Adjoa?" she asked, slightly out of breath and suddenly
embarrassed by the possibility that this person only looked
like her former masseuse. After all, it had been—what?—
eight years since they'd last seen each other.

The woman looked at her with raised eyebrows but nodded her head. "Yes?"

Janice held out her hand. "I'm Janice. Remember? From
Abidjan?"

Adjoa stared at Janice's face for several moments, her eyes lingering on her hair. Janice fought the impulse to pat at it to see if a leaf or something had been caught in the strands, until Adjoa finally reached out to shake her proffered hand.

"Of course, Madame Janice."

Janice smiled. "Oh, please, Adjoa. Have you forgotten that it's just plain Janice? When did you leave Abidjan?"

"It's been almost eight years."

"Then you left soon after me. Do you still give those great massages?"

"No, I own a beauty salon now," Adjoa said, pointing at the shop behind her. Squeezed between a tailor shop and a store that sold bathroom fixtures, the salon's façade was painted pink, with a single large window displaying plastic bottles of hair products on the inside ledge.

"You own this? Congratulations!" Janice was pleased but not surprised by Adjoa's success; she'd always been reliable and serious. Though they hadn't actually become friends during the half year they'd known each other in Abidjan, Janice had enjoyed Adjoa's visits—not just for the massages but because she'd been the only African there with whom Janice could speak English.

Janice studied the salon's sign, an Adinkra symbol that she didn't recognize painted alongside large curved letters that spelled out PRECIOUS BROTHER SALON. She guessed the name referred to Adjoa's twin brother, who'd lived with Adjoa in Abidjan; Adjoa had once mentioned that she and her brother were saving money to open a salon.

"I like the name," Janice said. "Tell me, how's your twin doing?"

She watched, dismayed, as Adjoa's face fell and her features turned slack and expressionless. It was the same stoic expression Janice had seen many times before, the look on her Senegalese friend's face when her husband took a second wife, the face of a Central African woman she'd met at a health center hours after her baby had been stillborn.

"Kojo died eight years ago," Adjoa said, in a subdued voice. "In Abidjan, before I left."

"Oh, Adjoa, I had no idea. I'm so sorry."

"Thank you," Adjoa answered, her voice mechanical.

Janice had lived in Africa long enough to know not to fill the awkward silence by asking what Adjoa's brother had died of. Sometimes the family didn't even know, or they didn't want other people to know. It didn't make any difference, anyway—of the myriad ways a person could die in Africa, they all ended the same.

Adjoa was silent, watching the traffic pass by, and Janice felt bad for having brought up a topic that obviously still pained her former masseuse.

"I'm sure Kojo would have been very proud to see the salon," she finally said, trying to sound neither overly cheerful nor overly glum.

Adjoa looked up at her and nodded, even attempted a smile. "Yes, I think so, too."

A peek at her watch made Janice realize she was now running late for her meeting. "Listen," she said, "I have to go, but next time I'm in the neighborhood, I'll be sure to stop by for a pedicure, okay?"

The least she could do, she decided, was to give Adjoa some business.

Adjoa watched Janice rush back to the car, painted with the logo of an African map and two shaking hands. Would she really come back again? Adjoa took a deep breath. It was too much—seeing her again, being reminded of memories she'd tried so hard to forget. For nearly eight years she'd been rebuilding her life without her twin, the sharp edges of his secret—*their* secret—wearing down as gradually and imperceptibly as rain smoothing a rock. In that time, she'd created a successful business and started a new life by marrying a wonderful man. She was finally getting along with her family again. And now, out of nowhere, like a vengeful act of God, this foreigner had appeared and might possibly even return and enter her salon.

Once the car was out of sight, Adjoa turned and walked back into the shop, the bell fastened to the door making a tinkling noise as she entered. Normally, she enjoyed the sound—it always reminded her of her good friend, Gifty—but today it was unsettling, a harbinger of something she couldn't place. What if Janice did come back? Adjoa went to her station, opened the drawer, and began rearranging the combs and brushes, the curlers and various scissors that lay inside. She would have to act professionally, of course, as if Janice were any other client. But how could she do that, when her mere presence dredged up such awful memories, including the image of her brother's broken body?

Adjoa felt a hand on her shoulder and jumped. Her assistant, Yaa, stammered an apology. "I didn't mean to startle you," she said, "but we've run out of tea to serve the guests. Shall I send one of the apprentices to buy a box of Lipton?"

She paused for a moment before answering. "No, thank you, Yaa. I'll go buy it myself. The schedule's light for the afternoon—you'll be fine without me for a few minutes."

As she set off for the small shop nearby that sold tea, Adjoa wondered why Janice had seemed so pleased to run into her. Back in Abidjan, they'd never seen each other beyond the weekly massages. Maybe Janice was lonely, still living by herself in a large house. She'd always been talkative, even back then, even though Adjoa had known her for only six months. Janice had left the country soon after the robbery—no, she was not going to think about *that*.

Instead of the shop, Adjoa decided to go to the supermarket near her house—they had a nice selection of biscuits and she could pick up a few boxes while she was there. And why not pop in at home beforehand? She was her own boss, after all. The salon was in good hands with Yaa, and no one would ask Adjoa upon her return why it had taken so long to buy a box of tea.

She hadn't recognized Janice at first. She looked different from their days in Abidjan, with so much of her hair

turned gray. But eight years had taken a toll on Adjoa, too.
Nobody could dodge the passage of time.

Adjoa turned onto her street and walked toward the
house she and her husband, Tony, had purchased a year
ago. At the time, he'd insisted they should live close to her
work because of her long hours, and since then she was
grateful for the proximity of their home.

As she entered the house, the sounds of rattling pans and
the smell of *jollof* rice coming from the kitchen reminded her
of the presence of their cook, Joy. Tony, she knew, was at
work overseeing his fleet of cars for hire. Adjoa slipped off her
shoes at the doorway and crept to the guest room, where she
gently closed the door behind her and pulled a small locked
metal box from underneath the bed.

Sitting down on the side of the bed, she placed the box on
her lap and opened it with a key from her pocket. She removed
the contents, wrapped in yellowed newspaper, and carefully
unpacked two bundles, revealing a pair of carved Yoruba
statues—identical female figures with bulging eyes, beads of
carved shells strung across their hips, and headdresses deco-
rated with fading blue powder. The wood felt smooth and
cool against her fingers as it occurred to her, once again,
how crazy it had been to hold on to them all this time.

When Adjoa had first seen these statues, they'd been on
a shelf in Janice's house. A trick of light—or maybe their
flat hanging chests and the strands of beads that disguised
their private parts—had made her think back then that
they depicted a man and a woman. They'd made her nervous,

knowing as she did, that when a twin died, the Yoruba often made a statue of the dead twin to house its soul so it wouldn't harm the living one. Even though she hadn't yet suspected what Kojo was up to, she'd felt something ominous, a fear she couldn't name, as she eyed the statues on Janice's shelf.

And she'd been right to be afraid. Within half a year, Kojo died in police custody after a botched burglary, and Adjoa's life changed forever. How agonizing it had been to bury his body in Abidjan, knowing he should have been laid to rest in his own land, but how else could she have kept the truth from her family? His body had been too mangled to match her story that he'd died of malaria, and she'd owed it to him to safeguard his name since she failed to protect him when he was alive. She'd even been willing to take on, for her twin's sake, the distance that her lie had wedged for years between her and the rest of her family.

The sweet scent of dust and wood drifted to her nostrils. Adjoa turned the statues in her hand. The backs of both figures were worn smooth and shiny, as if someone—a child perhaps, or even a mourning mother?—had carried them tied to their back, the cloth rubbing against the statue. She hadn't noticed this the first time she'd held them in her hands, right after Kojo's death and soon before her return to Ghana. She'd been packing, going through their cramped single-room house, when she'd come across a slightly larger version of the same box that was in front of her now—how Kojo had hidden it from her was still a mystery. She'd taken the box to a locksmith, who'd forced it open, the sight of its contents making Adjoa's heart plummet inside her chest.

There were other items besides the statues in Kojo's box—a baby's shoe, a bottle of perfume, even a gold cross. None of the other items looked familiar to Adjoa, nor did they make any sense to her, spanning the gamut of worthless to valuable. But those statues! They weren't just evidence of Kojo's guilt in the burglary at Janice's house, they were proof of Adjoa's as well. She'd been the one to ask him, week after week, to drive her to Janice's; it was *her* fault he'd met Maurice, the guard at Janice's house who vanished after the burglary. After she found the statues in Kojo's box, after she went over and over his behavior of the previous several months, Adjoa concluded that the robbery at Janice's house had most likely been Kojo's first. She guessed his encounter with Maurice had been the gateway to his short-lived life of crime, and that meant she carried at least some of the blame—not just for the robbery but for her twin's death as well.

If the objects in the box were indeed from the heist at Janice's and the ones that took place afterward, why had he kept such incriminating items? As souvenirs or talismans to ensure future success? The locksmith had offered Adjoa 10,000 CFA on the spot for the items, but she'd left him with the broken box and its contents without taking his money. The only items she kept—and she still couldn't explain to herself why—were the statues she was now holding in her hands.

The following week, Janice ate lunch at her desk, picking at
the reheated chicken and rice she'd brought with her. Most
of the staff had gone to a nearby chop bar, and the office was
thought-provokingly quiet. Moving to Accra had been
more complicated than she'd expected. The last time she'd
moved had been eight years ago, before she'd adopted
Alemnesh, and it was a whole different ball game with a
child. They'd stayed in Dakar much longer than she'd originally planned—it certainly wasn't her favorite post by a long
shot during more than twenty years in Africa. She'd settled
into an unusual inertia there, in part because the project she
worked on kept being extended, and in part because Alemnesh liked it there, forming close attachments to her nanny
and her friends.

At the thought of her daughter, Janice wondered once
again whether she'd done the right thing by moving them to
Accra. Even though—after an initial month of tears and
clinginess—Alemnesh was finally adapting to her new surroundings, Janice didn't know how long they should stay.
Should they settle here as long as possible, letting Alemnesh's
tender roots push into familiar soil in a way Janice had never
been able to? Or would Alemnesh grow up more adaptable,
more confident, if she was exposed to many different envi-
ronments? Janice had even considered the possibility of moving to the United States, where her mother and sister lived,
but she knew that in her profession headquarters was just a

bureaucratic hamster wheel; the real work took place overseas. Besides, she felt no pull to go back, no yearning to
spend more than the few weeks she visited each summer.
Nor did Alemnesh, apparently. Each time they visited, once
the excitement of seeing her grandmother wore off, she inevi-
tably asked Janice when they could go home.

Janice remembered perfectly the moment when she first
held her ten-month-old daughter at the orphanage in the out-
skirts of Addis, the way her heart seemed to constrict and
expand at the same time. She would be solely responsible for
this small bundle of life, and she both welcomed and feared
that responsibility. As she held Alemnesh, she vowed that she
would do everything she could to help her grow into a fearless
and self-assured young woman, despite the reality of a world
that could knock you off your feet when you least expected it.
When one of the orphanage workers explained the meaning
of Alemnesh in Amharic—*you are the world*— Janice didn't
know whether to laugh or cry at the perfection of it. Already
the baby had become the center of her universe.

From then on, everything she did was for her daughter; all
the decisions she made factored Alemnesh into the equation
first.

And now they were in Accra, and somehow Janice had
to go about making it feel like something akin to home
for Alemnesh—and, if possible, for herself. She knew that
could only happen once they began connecting with people
around them. Janice took another bite of rice and pictured
the friends Alemnesh was already starting to make among

her classmates at the American school. Too bad the parents Janice had met seemed overly preoccupied with keeping their servants in line or decorating their houses just so—hardly the kind of people she could relate to. She hadn't had any success making friends with Ghanaians, either. They were polite, of course—sometimes cloyingly so with their *Akwaaba* greetings—but nowhere near as easygoing or jovial as the Francophone Africans she was used to. Oh, to be back where people regularly invited you to their homes for a meal or to a nearby *buvette* for a local beer. Or to sit among a group of women, as they braided hair and hennaed one another's feet, listening to their comforting banter about unruly children and unfaithful husbands.

Janice's hand stopped in midair, several grains of rice falling from the fork back to her plate. Of course! Why hadn't she thought of it earlier? Adjoa's salon. Mango Tree Avenue wasn't far away; Janice could get there in ten minutes. She could even go now, stay half an hour for a pedicure, and return in time for work. Energized by her spontaneous plan, she strode out of her office, leaving her food half eaten on the desk.

Ten minutes later, walking into the Precious Brother Salon, Janice was welcomed by an onslaught of smells—the flowery scent of shampoo and soap with an underlying chemical scent of something sulfuric, from a permanent perhaps. The bright sound of women's chatter coursed through the air. The size of the space was modest, but the white walls and startling cleanliness of the room made a good first impression. Across from a vacant front desk, two ladies sat in easy chairs, talking between sips of tea. Along the left wall, Adjoa and a woman wearing a pink smock tended to two women seated in swivel chairs. To the right, a customer sat under a dryer hood, reading a magazine. Three girls, also clad in pink smocks, were busy with chores, one sweeping the floor, another folding towels, and the third rinsing out the hair-washing sink.

Adjoa looked up from her station, but before Janice could greet her, one of the smocked girls appeared at her side. "*Akwaaba*, madam," she said. "How may we be of assistance today?"

"That's all right, Suzie," Adjoa called out. "I'll be right there."

"May I offer you a cup of tea?" Suzie asked.

"That would be great," Janice said.

Adjoa bent down to say something to her client and placed her scissors on the counter before she came over. "Good afternoon," she said to Janice.

"Hello, Adjoa. The salon looks great; it's so clean and welcoming."

"I'm glad you're pleased," Adjoa said, her voice all business. "You've come for the pedicure you mentioned last time?" From her swivel chair, Adjoa's client was watching them intently.

"Yes, if you can squeeze me in. I just happened to have a half hour free. . . ." Janice suddenly felt awkward and unsure of what to say. Suzie reappeared holding a tray with a mug of tea, a plate of sugar cubes, and a small cup of milk.

"You can take Janice's tea to one of the stations," Adjoa told her. "You'll be giving her a pedicure."

Suzie beamed, revealing a gap between her two front teeth, before she turned with the tray to the other side of the room. As Adjoa motioned for Janice to follow Suzie, Adjoa's client called out from her chair, "Adjoa, aren't you going to introduce us?"

Was it Janice's imagination, or did Adjoa hesitate? But then she proceeded to introduce her client as Comfort, and the customer seated next to her as Comfort's niece, Gifty. Then she gestured at the other hairdresser. "And this is my assistant, Yaa."

"Hello," Janice said. "It's nice to meet all of you."

The women smiled and nodded in her direction, and Janice felt compelled to explain that she wasn't a complete stranger, that there was a connection, however tenuous, they might build upon.

"I knew Adjoa when we were both in Abidjan," she said. "We ran across each other last week by chance—after eight years, can you imagine?"

Comfort looked at Janice intently. "Once you reach my age," she said, "you'll learn that there are no accidents. If you found each other again, there must be a reason."

But Gifty just laughed and reprimanded Comfort for being so serious. "Maybe the reason Janice's life has crossed with ours is so that someone will finally tell us about Abidjan. Adjoa certainly never talks about it."

Janice felt an immediate liking for Gifty. About Comfort, who was still looking at her appraisingly, she was less sure.

"Well," she said, "to look at the city, it's very impressive with its tall buildings; there's a good reason it's called the Paris of West Africa. But beneath that veneer. . . ." She shook her head and started over again. "Actually, to be perfectly honest, I really enjoyed living there until my house was robbed. I'm not sure I can give you an objective opinion anymore."

At the mention of the robbery, Adjoa made a sudden noise, a sharp intake of breath, while Yaa and Gifty shook their heads in commiseration. Comfort sucked her teeth disapprovingly. "You were robbed?"

Janice nodded. "At night. I was in the house alone, sleeping. I woke up to a gun pointed at my head." No point in telling them about being locked in a closet for eighteen hours, trapped and helpless, until her cook, who waited outside her house all morning, had finally searched for help. Nor did she have any desire to describe the nightmares she'd endured for years afterward—dreams that had only dissipated once she adopted Alemnesh.

"How frightening," Gifty said.

"At the time, yes," Janice agreed. "Afterward, I was just angry. My own guard was one of the robbers." She recognized the same flippant tone she'd used with her therapist in Dakar, as if she were talking about something that had happened to someone else. Well, she'd never been one to wallow in self-pity or cave in when things got tough. And her determination had gotten her through to the other side. Why, she hardly thought of it anymore.

Comfort sucked at her teeth again, "Such a shame."

Adjoa interjected by calling over her shoulder, "Suzie, is the footbath ready?"

"Yes, please," the girl said, and Adjoa motioned Janice across the room to one of the hair-dryer stations, at the foot of which Suzie had placed a plastic tub of water. As Janice settled into her chair and removed her sandals, she felt someone watching her—her radar honed by years of living as a white person in Africa. She looked across the room and noticed that although Comfort and Gifty had their backs to her, their eyes were trained on her in their mirrors. Janice smiled at them, and was rewarded by their reflected smiles.

"So, do you have any children?" Comfort asked Janice in a conversational tone.

"Comfort—" Adjoa started, then stopped.

"What?"

"You have to excuse my Auntie Comfort," Gifty said, laughing. "She's never been afraid to ask personal questions."

Janice joined in with Gifty's laughter. She was used to this being the first question Africans asked—women especially. Men were more likely to ask if she was a Mrs. or a Miss.

"I don't mind at all," she said, as she lowered her feet into the warm water to let them soak. "And yes, I have a daughter. She's six years old."

"She's still young, then," Comfort said. "Mine are all grown. I have one son who lives in America. I visited him once, right after his first child was born. He lives outside your capital—maybe you've met him? His name is Ekow, but they call him by his Christian name, Peter."

Janice smiled. It still amused her how many Africans thought of the United States as if it were a village where everyone knew each other. "I'm afraid it's been more than twenty years since I've lived in the States."

Before Comfort could respond, Gifty changed the subject. "Tell us, Janice, what does your husband do here in Accra?"

"I don't have one, actually," Janice said. People often assumed that if she had a child, she must be married. "None of my past boyfriends worked out, and now that my hands are full with raising my daughter, I've stopped looking."

"You never know," said Gifty. "It might still happen. I was forty when I married Samuel, and we were blessed with a baby boy."

"What about you, Adjoa?" Janice asked. "Any children?"

"No, none," she answered, without looking up from Comfort's hair, a tone of resignation in her voice—or was it sadness? Once again, Janice felt like kicking herself for having brought up a topic she shouldn't have. She knew how important it was in African culture for women to bear children. Would it be so hard to keep her mouth closed sometimes? Then again, she'd been asked the exact same question by Comfort.

"Tell her about Tony," said Gifty, then promptly proceeded to tell Janice herself. "Adjoa was married a year after
me, to a very nice man named Tony. He's a successful business owner, just like her—he owns a fleet of cars for hire."

Janice flexed her toes in the water. "He sounds like a
perfect match."

"Gifty," Comfort said, "you talk about husbands as if
they were a necessity. Sometimes, in fact, they're more work
than they're worth."

Comfort's comment launched a good-humored debate
with Gifty about the value of husbands compared to the
effort they required. Janice, Adjoa, Yaa, and even the apprentices added their input to the banter. Laughing along with
the other women as Suzie began massaging her feet, Janice
chided herself for her earlier assumption that Ghanaians
were unfriendly. With the exception of Adjoa, who seemed
distracted and solemn, these women were just the kind of
company she'd been missing since she'd arrived.


It was clear to Adjoa that Comfort and Gifty had taken a
liking to Janice, especially when they insisted that Janice
come back for pedicures during their weekly time slot for
touch-ups. By Janice's second visit, Adjoa understood there
was nothing she could do to discourage it. On her third visit
to the salon, Janice brought along her daughter, Alemnesh,
who it turned out had been adopted from Ethiopia. She was
a sweet child, a slight girl with wavy black hair and skin the

color of tea with milk. The following week, when Janice brought Alemnesh again, Tony happened to pop in after dropping off a client. Since it was a particularly busy day, he stayed to keep an eye on the girl, entertaining her with a story Adjoa had heard a long time ago, about a frog with two wives, both of whom prepared him a wonderful soup.

"If I go to my first wife for the soup, my second wife will be sorry and angry," Tony said, in a deep voice meant to imitate a frog's. "If I go to my second wife, my first wife will be sorry and angry, too. Where shall I go?"

From her seat, Comfort muttered, "He should have thought of that before he took a second wife."

But neither Alemnesh nor Tony seemed to have heard her. "So what did he do?" the girl asked.

"Well, he sat and thought for a long time. And he stayed at home and began to cry: 'Oh! Where shall I go, where shall I go?' Now, when you hear the noise frogs make—*gaou, gaou, gaou*—you know that it means, 'Where shall I go? Where shall I go, go, go?'"

Alemnesh laughed and clapped her hands, encouraging Tony to launch into a different story, this one an Ashanti tale about Anansi, the mischievous spider. The sound of the child's girlish laughter made Adjoa's heart twist into a tight lump in her chest. Three years of trying to have a child had resulted in just a single pregnancy that didn't take. She'd been thirty-nine years old when she and Tony married—she understood it was harder for a woman to get pregnant in her forties, but she'd still assumed it would only be a matter of

time. Tony, always kind, claimed he didn't mind—he'd
already had two sons in his youthful days, one with a child
of his own. In the end, of course, it was God's will. But
now, watching Tony with Alemnesh, Adjoa felt a painful
glimpse of what they could have had if she'd been able to
carry her baby to term.

Adjoa looked into her mirror and caught sight of Janice
on the other end of the room, smiling at her daughter and
Tony. When Janice looked up, their eyes caught for a second in the mirror, and Adjoa quickly turned away.

As much as the sight of the child tugged at one loss, the
sight of the child's mother tugged as hard on another.
Every week it was like this: as soon as Janice appeared, Adjoa
thought of Kojo, and the weight of the truth bore down on
her like a heavy yoke. Instead of enjoying the weekly appointment with Comfort and Gifty as she used to, she now dreaded
it, knowing that Janice would be there, too. She knew she
acted differently around Janice—more than once, Gifty had
asked why she was so quiet. Despite Adjoa's discomfort, or
maybe because of it, Janice seemed to make an extra effort to
bring up topics Adjoa might want to talk about, asking how
Tony was doing, what it was like running a business, or even
who her tailor was. The nicer Janice was, the worse it made
Adjoa feel.

With each visit, she sensed Janice trying to burrow her
way into her life, inch by inch like a tiny worm, trying to create some kind of a friendship. And yet, Adjoa knew that a
friendship was impossible. If only she'd taken buses to Janice's

house instead of asking her brother to drive her those years ago . . . but it was useless to think like this; she couldn't go back and change things. The only choice she had now was whether or not to tell Janice the truth. But what would happen if she did? Janice would surely be angry, she'd probably tell Comfort and Gifty, who in turn were likely to tell Adjoa's family, raking up painful memories for all of them.

But not telling her was turning out to be more difficult than Adjoa had imagined. Every time she returned home after one of Janice's visits, Adjoa felt an irresistible pull to the contents of the box under the guest bed, as if the twin statues beckoned her. When Tony was busy elsewhere in the house, she stopped in the guest room to touch them. She sat on the bed and held them, one in each hand, weighing one against the other, as if the slightest difference in their weights might give her the answer she needed.

One evening, after Janice had come to the salon again, Adjoa asked Tony, "If you had a friend, and someone you loved hurt that person, are you obliged to tell your friend?"

They were eating dinner, a meal of boiled rice with Joy's palaver sauce—Tony's favorite, though Adjoa didn't particularly like the taste of cocoyam leaves. He stopped chewing and looked at her, bewildered. "What are you talking about?"

Adjoa sighed. She would have to be clearer without being *too* clear. "I'm asking for a friend who comes to the salon," she said. "She's trying to decide what to do, so she asked me . . . you know how clients always talk about personal things to their hairdressers—" She could hear herself overexplaining and stopped.

Tony made a grimace as if he'd just bitten down on a hot pepper. Like most men, he wasn't keen on talking about personal things, as she'd called it.

"It's a simple problem, really." She plowed ahead, though she was afraid she was about to make it sound less simple than she'd have liked. "This woman—my client—happens to know that her sister stole something—a pair of shoes, actually—from my client's friend, who's not a close friend, just someone she's getting to know. But the other woman has no idea who stole her shoes. And the sister is gone . . . abroad, and this woman, who is my client, she's wondering if she owes it to her friend to tell her because the . . . friend was very upset when the shoes were stolen, and not saying anything seems to be getting in the way of the friendship."

When Tony's only answer was a dazed blink, Adjoa added. "The question is simple. I'm asking whether she has a bigger obligation to her sister or her friend. Should she tell the friend what her sister did?"

Tony placed his fork on his plate and leaned closer to Adjoa. "Tell me, does this question have anything to do with the box under the guest bed?"

Adjoa felt her mouth drop open, then quickly closed it again. She stared at her husband.

"I haven't looked inside, in case you're wondering," he said. "I assume you locked it because I wasn't supposed to see it. You've been spending so much time in the guest room lately that I had a look around the other day and found the box."

"I had no idea you'd noticed."

Tony shrugged and picked up the fork again. "You ladies always complain we men don't notice things, but we're not as dim as you seem to think."

"I've never thought of you as dim, Tony. Why would I ask for your advice if I thought that?"

Instead of answering her, Tony put another forkful of rice and sauce into his mouth and waited for her to continue, his eyebrows raised. It was a mannerism that always reminded her of Kojo—Adjoa had seen that look on her brother's face countless times, usually when he was about to ask for something. Looking at the same expression now on Tony's face, Adjoa knew she couldn't keep the truth from him any more than she'd been able to keep anything from her twin.

"It's to do with Kojo," she blurted out, before she could stop herself. "He didn't die of malaria. I lied about that—to you and to my family, for which I'm very sorry—but I did it because what really happened was that he was killed by the police after he'd robbed a house—after he'd robbed several houses, in fact."

Tony looked surprisingly calm, so she took another breath and continued. "I should have seen it coming. I should have been more vigilant and made him come home. . . ."

She felt her throat close up and had to pause for a moment to swallow.

"But I didn't, and it happened. And I couldn't bear the thought of his ruined name, so I lied. And now I'm keeping the truth from Janice—you remember, the mother of the little Ethiopian girl you took a shine to?—even though that woman has always been kind to me, even in Abidjan. You see, hers was the first house he robbed, and he took two statues from there that I found after he died and I've kept them all this time—that's what's inside the box. I don't know why I've kept them when they're just a terrible reminder of everything that happened."

Tony's head cocked to the side. "I see," he said.

"And now," Adjoa said, "you're probably wondering how your wife could have kept something like this from you all this time."

To Adjoa's surprise, Tony's mouth broke into a smile, a piece of cocoyam leaf caught between his teeth. "Not at all," he said. "I was actually thinking about what you said about not knowing why you kept those statues."

Adjoa stared at her husband.

"It is possible, isn't it," he continued, "that you held on to them so you could return them to their rightful owner someday?"

As she let Tony's words sink in, Adjoa marveled at how easily he'd accepted the truth, how readily he'd forgiven her lie. What an uncomplicated view he took of the world. She watched him take another bite of dinner as if their conversation had been as typical as any other, as if the events she'd just recounted were perfectly ordinary and understandable.

But would Janice be as forgiving as Tony? Tony, after all, hadn't been the victim—he hadn't been the one to wake up with a gun at his head. Still, it *was* possible that Janice might not react as badly as Adjoa had originally thought. Maybe Janice had even put the whole incident behind her in a way that Adjoa had not; she hadn't mentioned it again since that first day.

Trying to smile at Tony, Adjoa made a mental note to let Joy know that she could make palaver sauce as often as he wished.

Janice woke up struggling, her heart clamoring in her chest and begging for oxygen. Bolt upright and clutching at her covers, she took deep breaths and told herself that she'd only been dreaming. Still, her nightmare had been so vivid—the coffin lid closing over her, the man's voice threatening to kill her if she moved, the sudden, utter darkness and lack of air. The voice had sounded exactly like the one she'd heard that night in Abidjan, speaking to her in English with an accent not unlike the ones she heard here in Ghana. And there had been the musty, humid stench of the coffin that reminded her of her closet in Abidjan—the smell she'd come to think of as the scent of fear.

She stood up to pull aside the curtains and flicked open the louvered windows to let in some fresh air. Outside, a faint tint of daylight washed the black night into a deep shade of indigo, and she told herself again that it had just been a dream—but no, it hadn't just been *one* dream. In fact, there'd been three in as many weeks. The first one, she'd been able to dismiss as a fluke, even the second she'd told herself was an aberration. But three nightmares in less than a month meant they were back; there would be more.

Still trying to shake her jitters, Janice tiptoed to Alemnesh's room. The dreams had stopped right after the adoption, and for her to have them now, five years later—could it be a sign of something terrible that had just happened or was about to happen? She threw open Alemnesh's door, making more noise than she'd intended. In the faint light, Janice could see the shape of her daughter turn around in her bed and pull herself upright at the noise.

"Mom?" she said, in a sleepy voice.

"Yes, honey, it's just me." Janice walked into the room and stood by the side of the bed.

Alemnesh wiped her eyes and looked around the room. "What time is it?"

"It's still early," Janice told her, leaning forward to stroke her daughter's head, reassured by the scent of her no-tears shampoo. "And it's Sunday, so go back to sleep. I just wanted to check on you."

Alemnesh made a grunting noise and flopped back under the covers. Janice considered sitting on the corner of her bed, but hovering would only transfer her anxiety to the child—the last thing she wanted to do. Besides, Janice felt an impulse to check on the rest of the house. She walked barefoot into the hallway.

Why were the dreams coming back again after so many years? Did it have something to do with the conversation she'd had about it with Comfort and Gifty the day they'd met at the salon? She crept into the study, flicked on the light, and threw open the closet—nothing but a couple of boxes of files. Or was it seeing Adjoa again, and being reminded every time she saw her about the final months in Abidjan? Janice continued to wander from room to room—guest room, living and dining rooms, kitchen, peering into closets, under beds, even behind the floor-length curtains—but she found nothing but a lingering mildew smell that came either from the closets or the remnants of her dream.

When Alemnesh woke up an hour later, Janice tried her best to hide her persistent sense of unease. She carried through on an earlier promise to take her daughter to the swimming pool at the Novotel and watched her paddle around in her orange inflatable armbands. But after just ten minutes, Alemnesh—who normally loved the water—insisted on coming out and lying next to her mother on a towel, their arms touching as they soaked in the warmth of the sun. When Janice asked if she wanted to go into the pool again, she just shook her head, her mouth a straight, thin line. It was only when Janice suggested they order some of the hotel's stone oven pizza—Alemnesh's favorite—that her daughter visibly relaxed, her face finally breaking into a smile.

By the time they drove home, it was already midafternoon, and Janice was surprised to see a box-shaped powder-blue car parked outside the fence, with the words TONY'S HIRING

CAR on the side. Adjoa was standing outside the gate next to her husband, a plastic bag in her hand. Alemnesh, who recognized them from their last trip to the salon, called out excitedly, "It's Tony!"

Once the guard had opened the gate and Janice parked her car, she invited Adjoa and Tony into the house.

"Mommy," Alemnesh asked once they were inside, "can I show Tony my doll collection? Please?"

"I'm not sure he's interested, honey—" Janice started, not sure of the purpose of Adjoa's and Tony's visit or even how they'd found her house.

But after Tony exchanged a quick glance with Adjoa, he said, "Nonsense, I would very much like to see her dolls."

"Then I guess it's okay." At Janice's words, Alemnesh took Tony's hand in hers and led him down the hallway. Once they were gone, Janice motioned for Adjoa to sit down. She took a seat on the very edge of the sofa, the plastic bag on her lap.

"I'm sorry," said Janice. "I should have offered you both something to drink. What can I get you?"

But Adjoa shook her head. "Nothing, thank you."

For a moment they were silent, until both of them started to speak at once. "How did you—" said Janice, while Adjoa said, "I'm sorry for—"

They both stopped talking and looked at each other. Janice sat down on the other end of the sofa and started to laugh, but stopped when she realized that Adjoa was silent.

"What did you want to say?" Janice asked. "You're sorry for what?"

"I'm sorry for surprising you," Adjoa said. "And you're probably wondering how I found your house. You mentioned once that you live in East Legon and we happened to be in the area. One of your neighbors brought us here. I would have called but I didn't have your number with me."

"I don't mind surprises," Janice said. "At least, not pleasant ones like visits from friends."

The word *friends* hung in the silence that followed, and this time Janice held her tongue. Despite what she'd said, she could tell this wasn't a social visit; Adjoa had clearly come for a purpose. Could it be to borrow money? Not that Adjoa had ever borrowed money from her before, even when she'd lived in Abidjan and clearly had less means. The most she'd done back then had been to ask for a raise.

Adjoa cleared her throat. "You have a lovely house," she said.

"Thanks."

Adjoa shook her head, seeming to make a decision. "We . . . I didn't come just because we were in your neighborhood," she said.

Janice nodded. "I figured as much."

"Ever since I saw you again, I've felt that I need to tell you something. Only I didn't know how." She paused and looked down at the bag in her lap. "I suppose I still don't know how. It has to do with my brother, Kojo."

"Yes, Kojo, I remember him," said Janice. She pictured a handsome man, with an open, intelligent face, wearing his baseball cap backward.

Adjoa fumbled with the plastic bag and pulled out something rolled in old newspaper that she began to unwrap. "After he died, I found these in our house."

Even when Adjoa unwrapped the statues and held them in her hands, it took several moments for Janice to register that they were the same Ibedji dolls that had once been on her bookshelf in Abidjan. She tried to figure out how the statues—which she remembered vanishing around the time of the robbery—were reappearing eight years later on Adjoa's lap. Because they'd been so incongruous compared to the gold jewelry and electronics that were stolen—and because there'd been much more valuable African art left untouched on the walls and shelves—she'd never been sure if they'd been stolen as part of the loot or if someone else had just swiped them. Seeing them now, in Adjoa's hands, Janice wondered if Adjoa had taken them. Maybe she'd been drawn to the statues because she was a twin herself. But wait—Adjoa had said she'd found them in her house.

"I don't understand," Janice finally said.

Adjoa lowered the statues to her lap and kept her eyes on them as she answered. "When Kojo died, I found out he had been involved in some . . . crimes." She paused, and when she continued her words came quickly. "He was arrested, and the police killed him, and when I went to identify his body"—

she took a deep breath—"I barely recognized him." She raised her hands to cover her face.

Watching Adjoa's bent figure, the statues in her lap, Janice felt her heart racing as it had from her nightmare that morning. The voice she'd heard that night—the one with the accent—she'd always known it wasn't her guard's, because he was Francophone, and the accent had been decidedly Anglophone, a voice steeped in the legacy of British colonialism. That voice had been Kojo's, the attractive young man she'd met only a few times, who dropped off and picked up his sister at her house.

For a moment, Janice felt dizzy. All this time she'd been as trusting and friendly as a puppy, and Adjoa had been keeping this awful secret from her. This, then, must have been the reason for Adjoa's standoffishness ever since they'd met again; she'd had a guilty conscience all this time.

Adjoa hadn't moved, and Janice felt her heart slow down to its usual speed, the dizziness subside. In its place, she felt the old anger rise, like bile, from her belly to her throat. It was because of Adjoa that Kojo had even known of Janice's house; *she* was partly to blame, even if it was true that she hadn't known what he was up to until after his death. And Kojo—but no, he'd already paid for his crimes. Adjoa, too, had obviously suffered. Still, Janice was angry. It wasn't fair that after all this time the fear those two men had inflicted on her was still there, even this morning, when she'd been scampering around the house like a scared rabbit and trying—not very successfully—to hide her feelings of helplessness, to keep her fear from rubbing off onto her daughter.

Janice heard the coldness in her voice as she said, "You're telling me that Kojo was the other robber." Although her inflection came out as a statement, it was intended as a question, a last-ditch plea for Adjoa to tell Janice that despite all the evidence, she'd somehow drawn the wrong conclusion.

But Adjoa nodded her head, lowering her hands from her face. "I'm so sorry," she said, her voice barely a whisper. "If I'd known, I would have stopped it from happening." She picked up the statues and held them out to Janice. "I don't know why I've kept these all this time. Please take them back."

But Janice realized she didn't want them back. Accepting the statues would be tantamount to forgiveness, and they suddenly looked unbearably heavy in Adjoa's hands. They looked almost malignant, with their protruding eyes and unsmiling mouths. Adjoa's hands began to tremble, making the statues move as if under their own power. A long time ago, someone—who had it been?—had warned Janice that African artifacts were best left alone; they sometimes had powers—good and bad—that she couldn't possibly understand.

No, she did not want the statues; they were just *things*, after all, and things could be replaced. What Kojo and the guard had forever stolen from her was something else, a sense of peace, of fearlessness, an innocence, perhaps, about the dark recesses of civilization.

"Please," Adjoa persisted. "They belong to you." Her voice sounded strangled, as if her neck was being choked—by what? By guilt? Regret? Or fear? Well, join the club, then. Janice had certainly had her fair share, too, over the last eight years.

The sound of a high-pitched voice drifted in from the hallway—Alemnesh chatting with Tony. Janice looked up to see her daughter holding Tony's hand in the doorway, her girlish chatter cut short mid-sentence. She was staring at Janice with eyes that were wide and unsure. Janice tried to picture what Alemnesh was seeing: a woman she barely knew, sitting on the opposite side of the sofa with her mother, obviously interrupted mid-conversation. Did Janice look angry? Or did she look as afraid as Adjoa?

Janice turned to look at Adjoa, sitting ramrod straight on the sofa and watching Alemnesh and Tony. Instead of fear, there was something else in her former masseuse's eyes. A tenderness, a trace of concern—the expression on a mother's face as she watched her child climbing a few feet too high in a tree.

When Janice looked back at her daughter, Alemnesh was still staring at her wide-eyed. Even though she was just a child, she picked up on her mother's moods. And children remember things. Janice felt a surge of protectiveness, an adrenaline shot through her body. She must preserve in her daughter the very thing—call it innocence, call it trust, call it what you will—that Adjoa's brother had taken from her that night in Abidjan. Had probably taken from Adjoa, too.

Janice tried her best to smile, to look reassuring and calm. "Look," she said. "Look at what your Auntie Adjoa has brought for us." And then she reached out to take the statues from Adjoa—and found they weren't heavy at all.

# ACKNOWLEDGMENTS

I could not have written this book without the support of my teacher, mentor, and friend, Ed Perlman. In addition, Jennifer Gennari provided excellent developmental editing and advice on the manuscript. I'm also indebted to Abigail Kyei for her encouragement and her patience in answering my endless questions regarding Fante culture and Malawian names.

For input into early drafts of individual stories, I'd like to thank Bob Bausch, Mark Farrington, David Keplinger, Margot Livesey, Alice McDermott, Margaret Meyers, Alix Ohlin, and Julie Wakeman-Linn, as well as Michelle Brafman and the members of the Glen Echo writing group. *Ameseginalehu* to Tigistu Adamu and Marion McNabb, who provided me with more background on Ethiopia than I could glean from my visits. I'm grateful to David Everett for his steadfast support, Mike Landweber and Will Thomas for last-minute advice, Alisha Horowitz and Dana Lewison for final read-throughs of the manuscript, and Regina Coll—artist and nurse—for easing me through the final labor pains of bringing this book into the world. Special thanks are also due to my sisters and fellow creative souls, Esther and Marianne.

My deep gratitude goes to my agent, Maria Massie, for her graciousness and wise counsel, as well as Helen Atsma, Gillian Blake, Nicole Dewey, Melanie DeNardo, and the rest of the team at Henry Holt for their relentless efforts and support of my book; a debut author could not have been more blessed! I would also like to thank the literary magazines in which some of these stories initially appeared: *Bellingham Review, Connecticut Review, Cream City Review,* and *The Massachusetts Review.* For their generous financial support, I'm grateful to the Maryland State Arts Council, the Arts and Humanities Council of Montgomery County, the Ludwig Vogelstein Foundation, and the Money for Women/Barbara Deming Memorial Fund.

Finally, I'd like to thank my friends who encouraged me over the years and who, upon reading the first story in this book, planted the seed by asking what happened next.

etc.

extras...

essays...

etcetera

more author
**About Susi Wyss**

more book
**About *The Civilized World***

...and more

Esther Wyss-Flamm

Raised in the United States and the Ivory Coast, Susi Wyss worked for nearly twenty years managing health programs in Africa. She holds an M.A. in fiction writing from Johns Hopkins University and lives in the Washington, D.C., area. *The Civilized World* is her first book. ∎

I can't point to one particular experience that inspired me to write *The Civilized World*. Instead, it's a culmination of my experiences from the time I lived in the Ivory Coast as a child through my career managing health programs in Africa.

After completing my master's degree in public health, I worked for over a decade, traveling to more than a dozen African countries and living in two of them, before the notion of writing fiction even occurred to me. During that time, I listened to people's stories, paid attention to my surroundings, and watched the world around me. I listened to a Burkinabè friend complain about being hauled off to the police station in Abidjan because he wasn't carrying any ID. I watched two Ethiopian boys fight each other with walking sticks near the falls of Bahir Dar. As a Peace Corps volunteer in the Central African Republic, I came across a flurry of white butterflies on the road from the Dzanga-Sangha Park to Bangui, and was struck by how much they looked like white snow. Maybe that was the beginning.

Or maybe it goes back further than that. Every writer needs skills of observation, and mine were honed in my childhood. I was always an outsider. As children born in the United States to Swiss parents, my sisters and I spoke Swiss-German at home. I didn't fit in at school—I wore the same clothes two days in a row, even my lunches of liverwurst on rye bread seemed all wrong. When my family moved to Abidjan, Ivory Coast, for three years, I was more of an outsider than ever, but I didn't feel the same pressure to blend in. Then we returned to the United States, and I felt like an impostor again. I learned to scrutinize my peers as a means to fit in—

Yes, famines exist, as do civil wars and AIDS. But people still live their lives, with the same joys and frustrations and desires all of us experience.

skills of observation that would also serve me as an adult in my international career, and, finally, as a writer.

When I began to write fiction as a way to explore my impressions of Africa, I consciously tried to represent the Africa I know and love, not the sensationalistic one people hear about in the media. Yes, famines exist, as do civil wars and AIDS. But people still live their lives, with the same joys and frustrations and desires all of us experience. I pictured characters who were like people I'd known, often struggling, sometimes succeeding—both supported and held back by their rich traditions.

By the time I wrote "Monday Born," the first story in this collection, I'd almost completed another master's degree, this one in fiction writing. Carving out writing time between trips overseas, I then wrote "A Modern African Woman." Another year passed before I received a visit from a Ghanaian friend who had moved to Malawi and told me about some of the Malawian names she'd heard. In Ghana, names are considered self-fulfilling, so she was shocked to hear people called Nobody, Why, and Grief—or, nonsensically, Address, Square, and Tonic. I knew she'd given me the seeds of a story, but it wasn't until later that the voice finally came to me to tell it—that of Ophelia, an expatriate woman with an obsession for names that masks a personal sorrow.

Around this time, *Connecticut Review* published "Monday Born." Several of my friends who read it complained that it left them hanging—they wanted to know what happened next to Adjoa and Janice. I looked over the three stories I'd written, and realized I, too, wanted to know what happened to the five characters in them. In what ways and what settings might their lives continue to intersect?

By this time, I'd decided to take a two-year hiatus from my job to write full time and finish a manuscript. I wrote the remaining stories over eight months, the characters becoming more layered with each story and asserting themselves as their lives took them in directions I hadn't anticipated. By the time I came to the last story, I knew I had to return to the beginning—to Adjoa and Janice and a pair of statues that had foreshadowed their misfortune. I knew, too, that this time the statues would serve a more noble purpose, and that the story would end on the same note of hope I have not just for my characters, but for Africa, as well. ■

1. The main characters in *The Civilized World* are all women. What common bonds do these women share? What divides them?

2. Ophelia discusses the power of names with Philip, telling him that a name "can leave a psychological imprint." Do you believe that's true? Adjoa lists for Janice the qualities associated with her name— do you think her name fits her personality? Do you think it's possible that she is who she is because of her name? What about the names of some of the other characters, such as Comfort?

3. What do you make of the mysterious pain Adjoa feels in her right arm? When does the pain seem to flare up most frequently? How does the loss of Kojo affect Adjoa?

4. Certainly there are some major cultural differences between life in the United States and in Africa portrayed in the novel; despite this, there are still also many overarching similarities. Think about Comfort and Linda, and Comfort and her mother-in-law, for instance. Can you think of other examples? What do these similarities seem to indicate about human nature?

**5.** At one point Janice thinks, "What did it mean to be civilized anyway?" She asks Bruce regarding the Baka women, "How do you know whether their quality of life is better or worse than ours?" What do you think? What does it mean to be civilized? Is any one way better than another? What do you think the novel has to say on this matter?

**6.** Janice feels most at home in Africa; Ophelia feels uncomfortable and out of place there. To what do you attribute this difference? Are they simply different women with different tastes? Or do you think they have different expectations for their lives in Africa, expectations that are in some ways self-fulfilling? Do you agree with Gifty's assertion that: "Life is like a mirror . . . if you look at it well, it will return the look"?

**7.** Watching Philip at one point, Ophelia thinks to herself that she "wanted to reassure him that she would change back into the person she once was. . . . Once the baby joined them, she would be the best mother and wife he could wish for, they would be a family, and everything would be fine." Do you think this is a reasonable thought? Does Ophelia truly believe it herself?

**8.** Think about Janice's relationship with Bruce, and Adjoa's with Kwame. Do you see any similarities between the two? Consider Ophelia and Philip as well. Do you think the women are trying to convince themselves that these relationships are something that they're not? If so, why?

**9.** Why does Marvin make Linda so uncomfortable? What did you think when Peter assumed that Marvin's friends were black? What does the situation with Marvin reveal about Linda and Peter's relationship?

**10.** Because the novel is structured the way it is, we are able to see many characters both through their own eyes and through the eyes of the other characters. How did your views of some of these characters change after witnessing them from another perspective? Did you find any of the characters to have particularly incongruous views of either themselves or others? How does the use of this technique further illuminate the characters?

**11.** Each of the main characters feels fearful at one point or another—this seems less true of the male characters. Do women generally feel more vulnerable to unsafe situations than men? In the final story, Janice vows to help her daughter "grow into a fearless and self-assured young woman, despite the reality of a world that could knock you off your feet when you least expected it." What role does this vow play in Janice's decision at the end of the novel?

**12.** This novel is made up of nine stories—what does this structure lend to the novel? The final story is the only one told from two perspectives—Adjoa's and Janice's. What do you think the purpose of this is? Do you think the ending is a hopeful one? ■

◆ *A Few Short Notes on Tropical Butterflies*
   by John Murray

The stories in this collection are powerful and dense—each one reads like a novel that's been condensed into a story. The settings range from India to the United States, the Himalayan mountains to the Rwandan border. John Murray doesn't go easy on his characters—they struggle and suffer and usually, though not always, survive. For me, the best books are those that make me think *and* feel, and this one does just that. He has also mastered one of the most challenging aspects of writing short stories: finding the right ending. Each time I reached one of his perfect endings, I had to pause and make sure I hadn't stopped breathing.

◆ *Breath, Eyes, Memory*
   by Edwidge Danticat

This book—about a Haitian girl who moves to the United States to be with her mother whom she hardly knows—also sticks in my mind as one that made me both think and feel. The lyrical quality of Edwidge Danticat's writing and the surprising, quiet moments of light make this book one I've reread several times. Moreover, I greatly admire how adeptly she renders dialogue in English when her characters are speaking in a different language. Without

etcetera

resorting to stilted direct translations, she nevertheless subtly makes it clear that the characters aren't actually speaking in English.

◆ *Swimming in the Congo*
by Margaret Meyers

I originally fell in love with this collection of short stories because the setting—1960's Congo—reminded me in many ways of my Peace Corps years in the neighboring Central African Republic. Since the stories are told from the point of view of a child, the daughter of an agricultural missionary, the narrator doesn't "exoticize" her African surroundings. Instead, the stories are first and foremost about growing up and trying to make sense of a complicated world.

◆ *Don't Let's Go to the Dogs Tonight: An African Childhood* by Alexandra Fuller

In this memoir about growing up in Zimbabwe, Malawi, and Zambia, Alexandra Fuller's writing is both poetic and visceral. Because she doesn't glorify anything— including her parents' drinking, the death of three siblings, even the African landscape—this book is a raw, heart-split-open narrative that held me hostage from the very first chapter.

◆ *Aya*
by Marguerite Abouet and Clément Oubrerie

In this graphic novel set in 1970s' Abidjan, the title character, Aya, is an adolescent girl more focused on her studies than chasing boys—much to the disappointment of her girlfriends, who resort to boy-chasing machinations that result in bittersweet comedy rather than true romance. Although this book shows a different world than the expatriate lifestyle I led in Abidjan during the same decade, I couldn't help but feel nostalgia for the "Ivoirian Miracle" years—before the current political and economic tribulations. ■